J.M. Varese is an American novel[...]
first novel, *The Spirit Photogra[...]*
critical acclaim. Varese has als[...]
literature and culture, and has served in various capacities, most
recently as Director of Outreach, for The Dickens Project at the
University of California for over two decades.

Praise for *The Company*

'[A] stylish Gothic chiller'
Irish Times

'Diabolically good . . . sinuously elegant and claustrophobic as
deadly Victorian wallpaper'
Kate Griffin, author of *Fyneshade*

'The neat set-up allows for a pervasive air of madness'
TLS

'Both subtle and relentless in its build-up of terror . . .
entrancing, entwining, and entrapping'
Hollis Seamon, author of *Corporeality*

'*The Company* creeps up on its readers before it so splendidly
pounces. The new master of suspense has arrived'
John Bowen, author of *Other Dickens*

'A crisp and austere work of Victorian gothic'
Eva Dolan, author of *This Is How It Ends*

Also by J.M. Varese

The Spirit Photographer

THE COMPANY

J.M. Varese

BASKERVILLE
An imprint of JOHN MURRAY

First published in Great Britain in 2023 by Baskerville
An imprint of John Murray (Publishers)

This paperback edition published in 2024

1

A CIP catalogue record for this title is available from the British Library

Paperback ISBN 9781399802659
ebook ISBN 9781399802666

Typeset in Sabon MT Std by Manipal Technologies Limited

Printed and bound in Great Britain by Clays Ltd, Elcograf S.p.A.

John Murray policy is to use papers that are natural, renewable and recyclable
products and made from wood grown in sustainable forests. The logging and
manufacturing processes are expected to conform to the environmental regulations
of the country of origin.

Carmelite House
50 Victoria Embankment
London EC4Y 0DZ

www.johnmurraypress.co.uk

John Murray Press, part of Hodder & Stoughton Limited
An Hachette UK company

For Adam, Gina, and Colette

Editor's Note

THE PRESENT WORK was discovered in an old abandoned house in Devonshire, long after the last of the Braithwhite children had passed on. The author, Lucy Braithwhite, was a person of great intelligence and kindness, known for her work in medical charities during the later years of her life. But why a young woman of her persuasion and station would feel compelled to record something of such unspeakable horror and obscenity remains a mystery. The story is as infernal as the ideas and events that it suggests. It should have gone to ashes with its author, and should never have been found or read.

The reader is therefore advised to proceed with caution. What tricks lie in this narrative are never evident or foretold. Indeed one of the only reasons to read it, aside from that of satisfying the most morbid of curiosities, is to find out, at long last, the explanation for the horrible thing – the *abomination* – that was discovered when the Braithwhite house in London was finally opened up again. At the time it was assumed that what was found upstairs was some macabre and unexplained relic of the family's complicated history. But now, with Miss Braithwhite having detailed the whole account herself, one can understand that much darker influences were at work.

That is, if one can manage to believe any of it.

The year, it appears, is 1870, for the writer makes some reference to events that took place during that time. One cannot be entirely sure, though, as there are so many distortions and evasions in this narrative that the grounding in any particular year must be treated with suspicion.

Tavistock, Devonshire
1903

I

FATHER BEGAN BRINGING us down to Devon when we were children. The business of the company drew him many times a year. 'Lucy,' he would say to me, 'you must take care to watch out for your brothers. Though John is older and Tom is slight, they are boys and they are bound to be reckless.'

He could be so grave when he gave a warning.

'There are bogs. There are dangers.'

But there were heavens too. The moorland – that heaven – beyond the Devon house was the place that as children we were forever wanting to escape to. We were children. We had freedom. Though I would always have less. And in the patterns of the rocks and hills, I remember the two boys running. Or rather, one is running, and one is falling behind, threading a path through the browning heather. He stops and turns his head. Our eyes meet and we smile. A hill and a boy – the simplest of patterns – and an immense sky that runs deep with no colour.

But that is a fanciful story, and not the one that I must tell. Because our family was the company, and the company was about something different.

We lived in a very fashionable neighbourhood of the city – not far from the Harley Street doctors, whom father often wished had taken up their residence somewhere else. Our house was a corner house, so that we had windows on two sides of some rooms, and that was important because it meant that the light hitting the walls could be extraordinary when the day was good. Father chose the house very carefully because of this. To him, there were two 'houses' to Braithwhite & Company. The counting house, which was down on the Strand, and the other house – the house we lived in. Both were ours.

As children, we of course all lived upstairs in the nurseries, alongside the servants. But some years after father died, John settled into one of the rooms on the first floor. It was father's old study, set towards the back of the house, just below mine, and once John turned of age, that's where we conducted much of the family business. The room's paper was of a dark emerald green, and it contained things shaped like leaves, and leaves shaping themselves into vines, and strange winding serpents that curved into rivers. It had been father's favourite. As a girl I'd seen angel wings somewhere in that dense forest, and John had picked out monkeys and pineapples. There was no telling what might emerge from any of these established relics – the intricate, deceptive patterns that our father's father had made famous.

But where to begin? I think not with a history of Braithwhite & Company, or a discussion of any of the wallpapers that made our triumph and our downfall, but rather with that last correspondence from our company's manager, Mr Luckhurst, and the other fateful letter that followed. That, to me, is where this wretched story begins – when strange stirrings within me, unrecognised at the time, began revealing the horrible course that I would eventually be forced to take.

How I loathe what I would need to become, but even then there was no stopping it.

I was twenty-four, and everything at that time was in predictable order: the designs for the new patterns had just been finalised; the sample books, as well, were being drafted based on the early designs; and interest from the London stores was not merely steady, but increasing, as our competitors had never been able to match our vibrancy of colour. That last bit had everything to do with Mr Luckhurst – or at least I thought so – who, over all these years, had kept Braithwhite & Company at the top of the heap.

Our dear Mr Luckhurst. How, as a child, I had adored him. And what would any of us ever have done without him? 'I trust you and your mother are continuing well,' he wrote in that last letter, 'and that John's health is as constant as we can expect it to be.' For while Mr L was not of a morbid disposition, he was also not a man who sweetened his words. Which makes more sense to me now, of course: the less he said, the better. In my childhood, though, he was the kindest of gentlemen – a confirmed bachelor who seemed always to have too much affection to give.

I remember once throwing my arms about him, and brushing my cheek against his soft, white whiskers. My seventh birthday, the year after we had lost father. The doll's house was the most exquisite thing I had ever received, fully furnished of course, and outfitted with samples of our papers. There were tiny dolls inside too – a family somewhat like ours. Mother and father in the drawing room.

A girl and a boy upstairs in their bedrooms. And on the top floor another little doll in its brightly papered nursery.

In the girl's room, on the second floor, the wallpaper looked delectable enough to eat – a mélange of peaches and berries and cherries, all intricately connected by melon vines. In my innocence, I touched the sun-like orange of one of the peaches, and some of the pigment rubbed off onto my finger. I put my finger to my tongue. Would the powder taste like peach? Would the flavour come from the walls? Were my new dolls to have so much deliciousness?

But no sooner had I licked the dust than I felt the air around me shift.

'Now my sweet Lucy,' Mr Luckhurst said, placing his hand upon mine, and moving it away from my mouth. 'You must never, ever do that.'

I looked at him.

'Never,' he repeated. 'You must never taste the papers, no matter how delightful they might appear.'

It was a different kind of scolding – one I remember more for its sympathy rather than its harshness. And of course it means something different to me now – something different from what it ever could have meant back then. He was protecting me from danger. His hand upon me, the gentlest of hands. Letting me know without knowing.

Mr Luckhurst was the man we trusted above all others. He was our saviour, and he was my favourite. But John was of course *his* favourite, and that I could not mind. Because John, after all, was the one who would some day run the company. This had been understood for as long as any of us could remember, and John, even then, couldn't help but reveal a distinct awareness of his own fate. How much more difficult it must have been then, for Mr L to observe John grow into a man over the years, and at the same time be forced to accept that not everything would turn out as it seemed. If Mr Luckhurst had one unfortunate flaw it was this: he did not always want to see what was right there in front of him because he lived, like so many respectable men of his time, strictly according to the rules.

In the end, that did not serve any of us well.

Mr Luckhurst was the public embodiment of the company. Or at least that is how father had established it to be, because Mr Luckhurst was trusted, and in business, as we had heard father chime time and time again, there was so little that one was able to trust. So it was no surprise then that when father passed away, Mr Luckhurst assumed his role in both 'houses'. He developed the most interesting partnership with mother, who listened half attentively as he explained this or that matter. And we could depend on him to spread the receipts from the counting house across the drawing-room tables, as he had often done when he had come to see father. Not that John or I, during those early years, could ever have made sense of any of those papers. The ever-presence, though, of so much business in the house impressed us with a deep sense of gravity for all things that surrounded the company.

Mother was still in good form during those years. And I mean the earlier years, before the trips to Devon stopped, and before I began having to care for her too. In both London and in Devon, mother was a kind of Mother of the Company – an important figurehead who did not transact business, but who influenced the company's workings by virtue of her association with father. I think that she enjoyed an unspoken partnership with Mr L, which is what makes me refer to the partnership as interesting. Or maybe it was spoken – I really don't know. I was too young to understand what was going on between them, or what the company's business was really about. During those early years I was instead noting moods and marking trends, as a girl of six or seven in a family like ours is wont to do. In any event, mother was quite soft, even before we lost Tom. It was she, for example, who would visit the bal maidens on our trips to Devon, and I remember her being overly concerned about the protective clothing we provided the workers. Perhaps involving herself in these more personal matters was her way of animating father's legacy – either that or her way of atoning for something over which she could never have had control.

In the end, though, as was the case with Mr Luckhurst, her rule-following would have its costs.

But to go on. Of my mother and Mr Luckhurst, my early memories are strongest in London, for whenever we were in Devon my heart was outside, in the fields and hills with my brothers. In London, my child's eyes did not see the sun rising and setting in the same way as it rose and set in the country. There were no purple or orange or pink wisps in the sky. No fields of frosty diamonds covering green blades of grass. In London, the colours were of a very different sort – blue skies and grey skies, or reds and yellows from the flower women, or the endless, endless panoply of hues from the fruits and vegetables in Covent Garden. And our walls and papers too, of course, which brings me back to the matter. Namely, our absolute reliance on Mr Luckhurst for the maintenance of – well, everything.

During the eighteen or so years since our father's death, Mr L had, like father, divided his time between the London and Devon offices. And so when Mr L was away from us, he naturally wrote more often. There were patterns. Mr L to dinner on Fridays, to discuss business with mother, and eventually with John, but also to maintain an honourable model of structure, which in our family was much needed. Mr L carrying in new display books, so that the business remained close to us. Then, Mr L to Devon, to ensure the efficiency of the company's mines, which ground through every season, day and night, rain or shine. And finally, Mr L's dispatches from the country, informing us of success and rarely of decline, week after week, until at last would arrive a letter providing a date of return, when the whole pattern would commence again, once he returned to London. If there is one thing that a destabilised household likes, it is predictability, and year after year, as our memories formed deeper impressions, Mr Luckhurst provided that to us, greatly.

And so, by the time I was twenty-four, and John was twenty-six, these patterns had become so established that one couldn't even see them any more. What we, or at least I, saw in the patterns was something extraordinary, which is to say – nothing. Because when you live with something for so long, and the purported beauty of what you're living with prevents you from seeing anything else underneath, you become less and less prepared for the arrival of something shocking. And as inviting – revealing even – as the colours of Braithwhite & Company's wallpaper patterns were, we could never have been prepared or awake enough for the wretchedness that was about to be.

The news arrived one night in a letter, just after the rain had stopped. The letter had been brought by a boy, not quite a man, wet and dirty. He resisted entering the house, but the air being so damp, Susan had insisted and pulled him into the entrance hall. When I arrived a moment later, the boy was already steeled against us, though try as he might, he could not hide his own shivering.

'He's from the office, miss,' Susan said.

'At this hour?' I replied.

The boy was indeed inside, but remained close to the door.

'If you please, miss,' he said, his arm outstretched. 'I was instructed.'

'Instructed what?' I said. 'You're all wet, boy, and you'll catch your death. Susan – bring a blanket and warm some water.'

The boy, sensing what I was about, waved his hands and said:

'Oh! No, no, miss. I was instructed. It's just this, and then I must go.'

His face had grown even more frightened at my suggestion. And now he offered the note up to me vigorously.

I took the envelope from his trembling fingers. I did not recognise the writing – simple strokes of black with no signs of flourish. It was not from Mr L.

'Who gave this to you?' I asked.

The boy looked behind me.

'Who?' I asked again.

'I don't know, if you please, miss,' he said.

'You're from the office?' I said.

The boy nodded.

'How is it that I've never seen you?'

'Well, miss,' he said. 'I just do as I'm told, and take what comes.'

I turned the envelope over in my hands, more curious about the messenger, if I'm to tell the truth, than I was about the message. The boy's stare was quite bold, courageous even, but it was an uncomfortable stare that held a gleam of terror, which in the moment I could not understand.

I looked down at the envelope again, turned it over, and tore the lip. There was a single piece of paper inside, folded in half. '*Dear Miss Braithwhite . . .*' the letter began, a scrawled message of merely two sentences. It was, as I had suspected, signed by one of the clerks – someone with no real understanding of what this news would mean to us.

I looked up at the boy and glanced back down at the letter.

'Miss?' Susan said.

But I could not look at her. Thinking on it now even, I can barely catch my breath. My eyes grow wet and my vision blurs. I choke – I cannot breathe. Susan catches me as I stumble. I drop the letter to the ground.

That is what I remember about that most unimaginable of moments: Susan, the misty boy, the floating away of the terrible letter. The letter is delicate – a feather falling to the floor. Though there will be nothing delicate about anything from now on.

Then I heard my brother.

'Lucy,' he said, 'what is the matter?'

He had come downstairs, undressed, in his nightclothes. I was still holding onto Susan, and I pointed towards the letter.

'I am . . .' I said. 'The boy brought . . .'

John moved away from us.

'What boy?'

Then he stooped to lift the paper, unfolded its wings, and read for himself that Mr Luckhurst was dead.

II

THE IMMEDIATE QUESTION, of course, in light of this horrid news, was not simply who would care for us, but who would now manage the company? John had recently suffered a severe bout, not that there was ever the chance of John taking Mr L's place, bout or no, anyway. And well, the truth was, that John was rarely *not* suffering from some bout or other, which was a constant reminder to us that father's most earnest wish, the thing father indeed seemed to have lived for – that a Braithwhite would always sit at the head of the company – was not to be. I'm sorry to say, that even as a girl I understood that this was something that weighed heavily upon John. We never discussed it. If someone referred to it, we buried it. My duty, from the very beginning, was to bury those kinds of things, and help John maintain, as best as I could, whatever strength he might possess.

Well, he was strong, despite what his doctors might say, and what everyone liked to think. He was strong to me, my brother, when we were out there in the hills, throwing small chunks of stone at shapes on the horizon. I remember a day when he ran far ahead of us. He kept going. I was but ten or eleven, and I was afraid, even though our feet knew the terrain. We were in a flatter, boggier part of the moor, where one had to watch one's step to avoid being swallowed up. Far in the distance, at the top of one of the tors, was a large mound of granite, hunched over like a monster. Hunched, and portentous – and hungry. It was very, very far, but John was going to run until he reached it. And when I think back upon that day, upon his vigour, upon his youth, and even upon father's cautionary words to me, I am still ashamed at myself for doing what I did. For trying to stop my brother from being a child.

'No, John!' I cried. 'John, stop! You mustn't!'

He did stop. He stopped for me. Because, I imagined, he did not like to make me afraid.

But then he called me a silly thing and kept going.

'You stay there and I shall return with the pixies' treasure!'

We watched him go further, for forever it seemed, running towards the crouching monster. It had rained that morning so the ground was very soft, and I was frightened that John would grow careless, and sink into the mud. The sun was low near the ground and the pools amidst the grass shone like silver. Those distant monsters on the tor were nothing to the hidden swamps that might engulf us.

But he stopped. John stopped himself without my prompting. The sun hit the horizon, splintered, and sliced the hills. There was a dazzling burst of orange, and crystals refracted in the air. From that distance, further than we ever could have travelled, the monster leered back at us, but especially at John.

On the way home that day, we came across the carcass of some kind of large bird – a hawk who had come down to enjoy his mouse, I first thought, only to be ambushed by a devious fox. There was dried blood everywhere, mixed with clumps of feathers, and pieces of flesh already becoming one with the ground. How long these decomposing remnants had been there, I cannot say. Perhaps the monster himself had left them to rot, uneaten, as a warning for wandering children.

Yes, I realise my metaphor is obvious, and that in that moment I must have seized on the idea that something was coming for us. But to imagine it or anticipate it in the moment would have been too horrible. We were children, and the figures were yet too young to be formed.

The horror of Mr Luckhurst's death, then, was compounded by the always simmering horror of wondering what would become of me and mother and John without him. For not only was Mr L the one man on earth capable of managing the whole of the company, but he was the one man on earth whom we *trusted*. We had known – and loved – Mr L literally since the day we were born, and his sudden absence forced us to confront the darkest of futures. Over the past eighteen years we had been lulled into complete complacency, and for all the resilience of Braithwhite & Company, we had nothing in place to ensure our recovery.

At least not to our knowledge.

Of course, the company could continue without Mr L, and so could we. But not in the same way.

I spent all my hours sleepless that night. Mr Jayne announced breakfast early, and I went down with mother. We did not know whether or not to expect John to join us (he usually didn't), but to our great astonishment, he came bounding in, fully dressed, and with a robust, 'Good morning.'

We wished John good morning, but otherwise remained silent. That is, until Susan and Mr Jayne had left us. Mother spoke first.

'It's horrible. What are we to do?'

'What do you mean, mother?' John said.

John was strong, upright. I couldn't even remember the last time I had seen him like that.

'He did everything,' mother said. 'The man has kept our very lives afloat. All these years . . . all these years . . .'

'Now, now, mother,' John said. 'This isn't the time for theatrics. He was a great man. A great, great man. Trusted, scrupulous. But he was getting on. We all knew that. Something like this was bound to happen, sooner or later.'

'He was still young.'

'He most certainly was not, mother,' John said. 'He was ten years father's senior, and you can probably add ten to that, given how relentlessly he worked. He was tired.'

Mother squeezed her napkin. John was rarely so engaged.

'It is just hard to imagine,' I added. 'We've never known anything else.'

'That's true, Lucy, but you forget whose responsibility it is, ultimately, to run the company, whether Mr Luckhurst is with us or not. That has always been the case, even though . . .'

He stopped.

'I know, John,' I said.

The truth is that John had remained ever hopeful, despite the constant reminders that his only place was with us, at home. The problem was on the surface, yet we all knew what could not be said. That if we were to say it, John might suddenly turn morose.

We began eating. Susan came in again and went out. I stared absently at the walls. Our dining room was papered in the boldest of carnivorous leaf patterns, inspired by the eighteenth-century design from one of the drawing rooms at Hampton Court. I thought of it as carnivorous because the leaves were not soft but distorted, and always made me feel as if at any second they might reach out and devour me.

At last John said that he had already 'taken action' – that he had written to the office that morning to enquire about the state of things there. Poor John. As the head of our household and of the company, he had felt compelled to do something right away. But there was so little he could do. Mr L had lately been spending most of his time down in Devon, and any information sent to us from the London office, at least that soon, would be incomplete.

But what I knew at heart, and what I think John must have known too, was that the company would manage. The company had always managed. It was too great an institution *not* to manage. Father's father had built it that way, and it touched – perhaps influenced is a better word – so many people and so many lives, that for the company not to manage would have been inconceivable. When the world saw Braithwhite & Company, it saw the picture of our family – generations of artisans and entrepreneurs who had changed the very conception of what a house's walls could be. It saw bright colours and daring strokes and jungles of exotic patterns, and the luxuries shared by royalty, which because of our skill and reach, it could share in now too. But that was only the tip of the needle, the point that kept things sharp. There were the papermakers themselves, who toiled in our workshops, printing roll after roll on new machines the size of buildings. There were the accountants and the office clerks in both London and Devon, the stock-takers, the cataloguers, the veritable army of drivers and coachmen, all of whom ensured that Braithwhite's goods continued to flow into every corner of England – and the world – like rainwater. And there were of course all the miners down in Devon who blasted precious copper from the ore in our mines and extracted all manner of things to be used in our pigments. The company was not simply a company, you see. The company was a force essential to the course, the very ebb and flow, of many lives. It was larger than any one person or family. And it was the deep sense of responsibility to that ebb and flow that kept John unshakably committed, and me committed to John.

The company could not die. The company must go on. The company now needed someone else – but who?

The intensity of the pressure upon John was profound, as the weight of the entire company now rested on his shoulders. And since I felt what he felt, the burden rested with me too. I could not separate myself from John – indeed I never could. And again, while we did not say it, all of us there understood that despite how radiant John might have looked that morning, he could not run the company. The stress of engaging directly with the business would inevitably have sent him into further decline. Knowing this then, had Mr Luckhurst made for any kind of provisions? Or, if one were to think more optimistically . . . could the company rely on its well-established competency and efficiency, and sustain itself, at least temporarily, without the kind of supervision it was used to? I knew not to expect anything helpful from the office right away, as it would take days if not weeks to sort out Mr L's affairs in both offices. But then, to our great astonishment, not two days after the disastrous loss, we were to receive our mysterious answer. It came in a form that none of us ever could have expected, a form as strange as it was troubling – and beautiful.

III

AS A CHILD, I was the one afraid of the paper. So much so that mother was eventually compelled to remove any wall coverings, entirely, from my room. As you can imagine, this was a horrid thing for her to have to do. The daughter of a Braithwhite, in a room without wallpaper! It was a disgrace to father's memory, and something that made no sense to anyone. But at that early point in my years – I was twelve or thirteen – my complaints had reached their zenith. My skin itched at the sight of so many vines, and my eyes burned from the glare of all those little birds – finches or warblers or whatever horrible things they were, twisted and glaring, and waiting to peck me to death at night. I heard their sinister chirps in the mornings when the room was silent. I felt their wretched little claws on my bare little arms. I wanted to put them in cages and toss them out of my windows, but they were safe there, safe and fixed to the paper, frolicking and haughty and complacent.

I hated them.

She could be cross, our mother, but she was not cross during this episode, because even then she knew something. She had consulted the doctors – the very doctors father had so disliked – about my irregular outbursts and my visions. I was a healthy girl. My mind was clear and my blood was strong. There should have been no cause for alarm – or so most of the doctors still believed at the time. If it wasn't too much trouble, they said, and given my obvious adversity to the pattern, might we simply consider . . . removing it? After some resistance, mother finally relented. Susan took me out into the city one day and we returned to find the creatures gone from the walls. The following day, mother had my entire room painted over in a beautiful dusty rose.

Children have great power – a power that can sometimes be extraordinary. They will tell you things that no one else will tell you, because they see things no one else can see. This episode with my paper was, I remember, about two years before we lost Tom, and though he was only six at that time, he too had started to become anxious. From his bed upstairs he would stare at his own paper. His breathing would change, his body would shift, and small beads of perspiration would form on his forehead. I was the only one who fully understood, I was certain. Mother was too concerned with listening to the doctors to understand, and Tom's nurse, Mary Toole was – well, rather simple.

I cared for things. I cared for Tom. I cared for my doll's house, its rooms and its inhabitants. I cared for mother, during Tom and after Tom. And though I was but a little girl when father died, I was the one who looked after Henry, father's parrot, the only bird I ever liked. Our house was bursting with an employment of caretakers – Susan, Mr Jayne, old Mrs Dawes (downstairs), and Mary Toole at the time – and yet there was something ill-natured about the formula. Any lines of stability within the house had been drawn more by Mr Luckhurst than by mother, but because Mr L's presence was so irregular, the lines tended to twist. I remember once when I was fourteen or fifteen becoming enraged at Susan for bringing John's tea in without sugar. This was after Tom died, of course, and John had moved down to father's study, and though John was young and handsome and hopeful, his face was already showing the signs of his fate. He was in bed that day with what seemed like a mild cold, and Susan came in with his tea, and there was no sugar. It was unpardonable. Or at least I felt it as such, because John needed his comforts, no matter how small.

'Susan!' I exclaimed. 'You careless, careless thing!'

'I'm sorry, miss,' she said. 'I've been a bit distracted.'

Her eyes had reddened, but I didn't care and continued to scold her. She ran from the room and finally returned with John's sugar. Then she left us, head-hung and ashamed.

John became mine. He could not be mother's, because mother was not capable of having him. Mother was roaming about, and she was not well either, only her 'sickness' was compounded more by the persecution she heaped upon herself than anything else. Mother knew more than anyone, but she hid as much as she could. And so I was left there – amongst John, amongst mother, amongst Susan and the rest of them – the only one to draw lines, the only one to observe the patterns, the only one with the knowledge and power to assure that we would not lose another son, too. That was what was most important – John, and John's longevity.

I would do whatever needed to be done.

You can imagine, then, not just my relief but my *elation* at the – what should I even call what I thought it was? Solution? Gift? Blessing? – that appeared on our doorstep in the wake of Mr Luckhurst's death. It was a Friday morning in the middle of September, and we had all long finished breakfast. John was having another good day, was fully dressed, was even sprightly for the second day in a row. This was astonishing – I cannot stress how much – because it simply never happened. John at breakfast, handsome John, with his hair parted, pomaded, and a sapphire tie pin gleaming on his breast. In any case, as I said, we had finished breakfast and I was upstairs reading a poem in an old dusty volume by Mr Donne – the poem, I think, about the fish and the bait – when something must have happened down below. I heard no bell, or knock, or front door open, and to this day that remains something I have never been able to explain. I can only offer that I was absorbed in my poem, and perhaps lost in the golden sands that called to me.

All of a sudden the sun hit my eyes. I rose and went downstairs. John was not alone in the drawing room when I entered. There was another man there, by John, and near the window. He was a young man, John's age, perhaps a year or two older. A faint blush coloured his cheeks for a moment as he turned to face me.

'Lucy!' John said. 'I am delighted to introduce you to Mr Julian Rivers. He has come from the Devon office to help us manage things.'

'Mr Rivers,' I replied, offering my hand.

He took it, and something happened. The comfort we had all been longing for was somehow there, in his grasp. I will say it: the comfort *I* had been longing for, because even though the fate of the company weighed most heavily upon

John, it was I who would ultimately be steering the course of that unwieldy ship.

I immediately became more conscious of my dress. I had chosen it quickly that morning – not one of my best.

'Miss Braithwhite, an honour,' the young man said.

He was wonderfully handsome, with the most finely curved lips, clear eyes, and crisp hair. And there was something in his face that made one trust him at once. There was also, I dare say – and I am hesitant to use this word, especially now – an air of *innocence* about him. Yes, his stature was full of command, and his eyes possessed a quality that suggested that they had seen things, but the whole of Mr Rivers seemed wrapped in a kind of purity.

I will say it. I was taken.

'Mr Rivers,' I said. 'Thank you for coming up to see us. We have been, as you can imagine, quite concerned.'

'Miss Braithwhite,' the man replied, 'I do not need to imagine. I have been with the company for many years now, and you must believe me when I say that I share your concern – and your grief.'

Ah, that was it then. That explained who he was, and why he was here. He was one of the managers from the Devon office, and he had been one of Mr L's many protégés.

Susan brought in tea, bowed demurely, and went out.

'Lucy,' John said, 'Mr Rivers here is nothing short of . . . a miracle. He has been managing every aspect of the Devon operations under Mr Luckhurst's guidance for the past few years now.'

'And London,' Mr Rivers interjected.

'And London,' John added. 'Mr Rivers is acquainted with the London office as well.'

'More than acquainted, sir,' Mr Rivers said.

'Yes,' John said. 'Forgive me, Rivers. I'm not doing right by you. Lucy, what we have here is a manager who has been working alongside Mr Luckhurst, in every capacity, for going on ten years.'

'Ten years?' I questioned.

It was a bit unfriendly, but Mr Rivers took my meaning.

'Yes – I came to the firm when I was eighteen. Well, truthfully, some years before that. But Mr Luckhurst began training me in the trade as I came of age. He was like a father to me. He was everything to me.'

In his eye – that eye that held something indescribable – there was also the reflection of sadness, and regret. The sun shone fervently into the room. It was a bright day for us all, despite that larger shadow.

'He was everything to me, too, Mr Rivers.' I said. 'And to John. He was our father, when we had none.'

Mr Rivers glanced down. He needed say no more. He had been one of the many, like us, who had been 'saved' by the generous Luckhurst. He was an orphan of some kind, the son of friends who had passed, a youth who had shown promise, but whose hopes had been dashed by life's circumstances. He had been educated – perhaps Mr L had sent him off to school – and though he could not completely hide where he was from, there was something glorious in the way he spoke.

'Rivers and I have been going over matters, Lucy, and—'

'When did Mr Rivers arrive?' I asked.

'I arrived in London late last night,' Mr Rivers said.

'No,' I said, addressing John. 'The house. When did Mr Rivers arrive here at the house?'

'Perhaps twenty minutes ago?' John said.

'Yes,' Mr Rivers said.

Again, I was astonished at how I could have missed his coming.

'Ah,' I said. 'And you have been discussing matters.'

'Yes, Lucy . . . and from what Rivers has been telling me, we are primed for one of our greatest seasons yet. The orders from the London stores are increasing by the day, and the orders from America, are, well . . .'

'Like nothing we've ever seen.'

He said the words with a confidence that was disorienting. He was looking at me. Or rather, looking into me. I can only describe what I felt in that moment as something very strange – a vibration that was frightening and exciting all at once. No one had ever looked at me in such a way before, not even my last suitor, Mr Carmichael. Or if he had back then, I had not been able to take notice.

We paused, and then John said:

'Rivers has it locked down, Lucy. He really does.'

It all seemed so quick – much too good to be true – that 'another Luckhurst', or at the very least someone who knew all that Mr Luckhurst knew, and could do all that Mr Luckhurst could do, should materialise, as if from the very walls around us.

'Mr Rivers,' I said. 'It's a mystery to me that we've never heard of you. Over the years have you come to London often? I don't believe Mr Luckhurst ever mentioned your name.'

'I've been based in Devon,' was his reply. 'But yes, I have been to London, quite often. Mr Luckhurst felt it was important for me to understand the many differences between the two offices, as well as the similarities. Mr Luckhurst brought me often – quite often.'

And there was something in that, too – something difficult to explain. It was as if, in the way he said his 'quite often', he was trying to tell me that, while he forgave me, I should have been aware of that detail already.

He observed my mind working, and jumped back in.

'You both know that Mr Luckhurst had his reasons for everything. As I said, I've worked primarily in Devon. In fact, in recent years, the Tavistock office has been almost entirely under my supervision. And yes, while I've frequented London, many times, the Devon operation has been my chief concern. It is what Mr Luckhurst wanted, and this is likely the reason for why our paths may never have crossed.'

He was looking into me again, and he knew about our family. He knew that we had long since stopped travelling to Devon, to the house there. For all I knew, he himself had been living in that house. We had not been back to Devon since Tom, well – at least ten years.

'Ten years is a long time,' he said.

I stared back at him, stunned.

'A very long time, especially in the life of someone such as me, who was never meant to receive such opportunities.'

He looked away from me, glanced at John, and back at me again.

'I will not disappoint you.'

I did not want to leave John alone with him, but something was telling me that I needed to retreat. Yet if I am to confess the truth, as much as it pains me to say it, even now, *I* wanted to be alone with him.

I wanted to question him, outright, about all he had come to know, and all that he had seen. I desired to learn everything about him because Mr Rivers was a man who had seen, and heard, and tasted everything. The air of innocence I had first observed in him was false. I knew it. And the immediate intimacy with which he addressed me let me know that *he knew* that I knew it. There was something completely terrifying about the unspoken way in which he communicated. And yet, the whole picture that he presented seemed a thing of indescribable comfort.

I did leave them to 'discuss matters', and later that evening, when our family assembled for dinner – the stuffed partridge with cherry sauce that I had specifically requested for John – the effects of my brother's meeting with our new manager were plain. Yes, John had picked up, strangely, over the past few days, but at dinner that night the energy and enthusiasm he exhibited were something we hadn't seen in years.

'Mother,' he said, 'I'm telling you, his understanding of the business is exceptional. I grew up in the business, with reports from Mr Luckhurst since I was a boy, and yet, after one conversation with him, I feel as if I know only half as much as this Rivers does.'

'It does seem fortunate,' mother responded.

'It's more than fortunate!' John said.

He was animated, no signs of the old troubles on his face. His skin was clear, his cheeks flushed. His expression full of delight.

'Perhaps it is the remuneration this family is to receive after so much misfortune,' mother replied.

Neither John nor I responded. Mother often turned the matter thus.

'I'll tell you what's remarkable,' John said, moving on. 'What's *really* remarkable is his bravery around the formulas. He has ideas, Lucy – ideas that old Luckhurst never would have been courageous enough to pursue.'

'Not the colour formulas,' I said.

'Yes,' John replied.

I was sure that I had grimaced, and then realised that I must have looked contrary. But I could not help it. The last thing our family needed was anyone doing anything else with the formulas.

'Oh, I don't mean to insult our dear guardian's memory,' John went on. 'You know that, Lucy. You know I loved him. The company – the family – will never be the same without him. But Mr Rivers, you must understand, is, well . . .'

He was searching for the word.

'Fresh?' I said, reluctantly.

'Knowing,' John said. 'Mr Rivers is knowing.'

The potency of the effect someone like Mr Rivers could have on someone like John was now before me. I am quite ashamed that I hadn't entirely observed it while I was still in the room with them. You see, for a man like John, who had been denied his proper course in life, who had been denied proper access to the business, and even, I would go so far as to say, the world, a man like Mr Rivers was inescapably desirable. Mr Rivers would necessarily know things John could never know, would have seen things that John could not have seen. And yet, that common experience of 'growing up' under Mr L's tutelage, coupled with what I imagined to be Mr Rivers's unfortunate history, were elements that bound my brother to this man so quickly that I had missed it in an eye blink. It did make sense though – John's energy made sense. And, after so much illness, a lively John was such a good thing to see. The only point that left me a shade embarrassed was the mistaken perception that Mr Rivers's offerings of comfort had been primarily meant for me.

Later that night, alone with John in his room, I could not help but share in my brother's feelings of a heightened heart. It was as if hunger had plagued us, and then a feast appeared before us – a bounty the likes of which we never could have imagined. I did not understand how much I yearned for his lost spirit until I had seen with my own eyes that that spirit could return. And though I knew John's condition could not be permanent, to see him so refreshed after his connection with our new manager gave me a small thrill, even if I could not let go of my concerns.

But there was more.

Our conversation had momentarily stopped, and John was looking into the coals. I would not go so far as to say he was distraught, but at that late point in the evening, there was a definite turn in his spirit. I never liked to push John, because one never did truly know how he was feeling, but in those few strange moments of silence, something troubling had crept into his mind. He sat there looking at the fire grate for some time, his palms together and his fingers at his lips. The light from one of the lamps flickered on the emerald patterns behind him, and with furrowed brow he was the picture of our brooding father.

'John?' I at last said.

He did not look up at first, but pressed his fingers more intensely into his lips, before releasing his hands, and drawing one of them to his forehead.

Then he did look at me. There was worry there. The robustness and the redness still clear, but there was worry.

'I remember now,' he said.

The coals were glowing, and Henry, performing his bedtime preening in his cage, was casting a jitter of shadows on the wall.

'I remember,' he said again, shifting.

He did not go on, so after a moment I gently urged:

'What is it?'

He stared at the fireplace.

'Tom's funeral,' he said, finally. 'I saw him there – at Tom's funeral.'

'Who?' I asked.

'Rivers,' John said. 'Rivers was there. At the funeral.'

That black day ten years ago rushed back upon me. We had buried Tom down in Devon, with father.

'What do you mean, John?' I said.

'Of course,' he said. 'It only hit me just now, as we were speaking – the connection to Rivers, and why it felt so strong. I had seen him once before, only I didn't remember. But my elation at his appearance, that uncanny feeling that these 'right' things happen just when you need them to – that was all coming from a sense of familiarity that I was unable to pinpoint. It was itself uncanny – the feeling that went through me when he took my hand—'

'I know, John,' I interrupted. 'I felt something like that too.'

Henry made a little noise. I looked over at him. He was considering us. He had been witness to so many moments like this – memorable moments between me and my brother.

'So you remember him too, then?' John said. 'You remember him from the funeral?'

'No,' I said. 'But the strangest feeling did overcome me when he took my hand. As if he understood exactly what we needed, and that he held—'

I paused. I felt such a silly thing even thinking it.

'Held what, Lucy?'

I gripped my hands.

'Well . . .' I said. 'The remedy.'

Now I looked into the fire grate too, the shapes and patterns distorting themselves in the coals.

'I never spoke of it,' John said.

'Of what?'

'Of what I saw that day. Of seeing Julian Rivers at the funeral, though I had no knowledge of his name, or who he was then.'

'What is it that you saw?' I said.

'Now that I am thinking on it,' John replied, 'it is not so much what I saw, but what *he* saw. It was the way he looked at me, across the grave. He was standing there, at the back of the crowd, like some sort of apparition. There was something enthralling about him. The impression his face made upon me was . . . well, it was a—'

'Yes, John,' I interrupted again. 'An unusually beautiful face, I know.'

John rubbed his hand across his mouth, the recollection preying upon him.

'I can only explain what I experienced in that moment as a feeling of terror. But a terror that drew me in, and – this is so impossible to explain – would not let me go.'

John looked to me for some kind of confirmation as to my surprise, but nothing he was saying surprised me.

'You had the urge to run,' I said.

'Precisely.'

'And yet, you could not.'

'Yes. It was as if he were speaking to me, across the crowd. The lips did not move, but I heard him.'

'And what was it that you heard?' I asked.

'I realise this all sounds absurd – ridiculous. A preposterous fancy of my boyhood imagination.'

'It's not fancy,' I said. 'I do understand.'

'The look – it was an extraordinary and terrifying look. We locked eyes for that brief moment as the minister was imparting the final blessings. The look said that he knew me, that he knew everything about me.'

'Much like the feeling he communicated to both of us today,' I offered.

'It's true,' John agreed. 'He did communicate such a feeling today. And in it a feeling of comfort. But what I'm remembering is not at all comforting.'

'And why is that?'

'Because,' John said, 'as he looked at me that day, Mr Rivers seemed to be saying something else.'

I remained quiet, and at last John went on:

'As I stared back at him, there was something in his expression that said that he—'

John paused again.

'That he despised me.'

33

A sting surged through me. Had I not seen that too? Ah, but those long looks of comfort. The innocence, the knowingness.

'It was ten years ago,' I said. 'There were many people about, mother was upon us, and all our eyes were misty with the loss of our little brother. Can you be sure that this apparition you say you saw was in fact . . . Julian Rivers?'

John shook his head.

'There can be no doubt,' he said.

And he stared me down.

'Is it a face *you* could ever mistake?'

Then John did the strangest thing. He smiled – smiled at the orange glow that throbbed within the fire. Henry made a sound, as if he too were claiming part of the memory, and as he preened, the soft click of his beak seemed to be ticking along with our thoughts. Then I remembered something of my own from our encounter that afternoon. I had, as I stated, left John and Mr Rivers to discuss their business, but as I made my way out of the drawing room, I turned to catch a final glimpse of them. The sun was streaming in upon their conversation, and they could have been two brothers or friends. And then, just as I was closing the door, I observed something that, to me at least, altered the hue of their entire transaction. Mr Rivers touched my brother. Yes, as one might console another in deep mourning at a funeral, Mr Rivers raised his hand and touched the back of John's arm in a communication of sympathy – or affection. What they were saying to each other at that very moment I could not hear, but the effect of the gesture upon John was not inconsiderable. John did not recoil, or signal even the slightest retreat, but rather loosened under the warmth of the movement. I had already surmised that you could tell Mr Rivers a secret, and even if it were an awful one, he would not judge you, or reduce your possibility. Mr Rivers made anything possible, I thought, which is why both John and I had become so intrigued. But this small and private interaction that I accidentally observed told me something else: that from the mysterious bag of tricks Mr Rivers held in his possession, he was able to offer my brother a kind of comfort that I had never been able to give.

IV

THE NEWS WAS good over the next two days, and Mr Rivers paid us an uncustomary visit that Sunday. Though his original intent had been to return to Devon, he would be remaining in London for the next few weeks. There was a great deal he needed to look into at the counting house, he said, and though he anticipated no problems, he wanted to be sure that the affairs for the coming season were all lined up. What 'affairs' these were exactly, I did not know, and I'm not sure John did either, because neither of us had ever been embedded in the business enough to know what all the tables added up to, or exactly how many were in our employ. Yes, it's true that John, as his health allowed, was involved in the larger matters of the company and the more important points of discussion. But the daily ins and outs tracked by Mr L – and now Mr Rivers – lived in a more obscure world that had been for the most part out of our reach.

Mother encountered him that day, or perhaps I should say he encountered mother, for when she came into the drawing room and first saw him sitting next to John, she displayed none of the visible appreciation for his arrival that John and I had expressed. She had known he was coming, but hadn't taken any extra care, and the dress she wore was her old blue one, the hem of which I had been meaning to fix.

'We are most grateful that you have come to take the place,' she said, sitting, 'of one who was so impossible to replace.'

'It is my duty,' Mr Rivers said, 'my most profound duty, to step into the place Mr Luckhurst long prepared me for, and to serve this family as he did.'

'He was faithful,' mother said, stoically.

'Indeed, Mrs Braithwhite – a man of great fidelity.'

'There are choices, Mr Rivers, and Mr Luckhurst knew how to make them. When I say that he was faithful, I am not just referring to his faithfulness to the company. He was faithful to his larger sense of duty – to this family.'

'For a house as successful as Braithwhite & Company,' Mr Rivers said, 'the choices are many – and difficult.'

Mother looked about the drawing room, and then returned her attention to him.

'And when you say "long prepared", Mr Rivers, by that you mean—'

'I have been with the firm some ten years now,' Mr Rivers interjected. 'I hope you'll forgive my saying so, but Braithwhite & Company has been . . . a home to me.'

Mother nodded. She was not yet seeing the potential he offered, but of course she eventually would.

'You're from the west country,' mother said.

'I am, ma'am. From Devon.'

'From?'

'My family . . .' he hesitated, 'comes from Morwellham.'

'Ah – in the shipping business then?'

'No, ma'am. They are no more.'

We remained quiet. Then John said:

37

'Morwellham . . . Father took me down to the quay there once – on one of the copper runs. Charming place. The river is very beautiful there.'

'Yes,' Mr Rivers said, 'quite so.'

We conversed for some more time, and I was conscious of mother's sombreness, and the effect it might be having on Mr Rivers. Mother had never been inclined to go out of her way to make anyone comfortable, but Mr Rivers was unflappable, and accommodated her every question. Already, it seemed, he was starting to belong to our house as much as anything else inside it. At one point, he rose and went over to Henry, and reached his finger through the cage to stroke the bird's neck.

'This bird is marvellous,' he said. 'I've never seen such green.'

'Yes,' mother said. 'He was a gift to my husband from Mr Smith, at Kew Gardens.'

'He's getting on, Henry is,' John said. 'Mr Smith brought him back for father in 'fifty, I think?'

'Yes,' mother said. 'Twenty years ago. It was a trip to Jamaica, to collect specimens.'

'An extraordinary creature,' Mr Rivers said. 'The colours are marvellous. They give me ideas.'

He continued to run his finger through the feathers around Henry's neck, stroking and scratching the bird's skin, which put Henry into a kind of reverie. I had never seen old Henry so calm. The bright scarlet feathers around and below his beak rippled beautifully under Mr Rivers's touch.

When it was time for Mr Rivers to depart, John escorted him downstairs. Mother retreated to her room and I watched through the lace curtain as Mr Rivers emerged from the portico, tipped his hat to my brother, and turned to his horse. The horse had been secured to a post, and was standing there obediently. What a fine form Mr Rivers cut in his well-fitted coat – a man who could rule the world! And it was not a stretch to think such a thing, because Braithwhite & Company was our world, and Mr Rivers would now rule it. Mother was upstairs but even so I could hear her thoughts – that no matter how handsome or commanding Mr Rivers might appear, his mother had been a bal maiden, she was sure of it. What later caused her to dismiss these prejudices I would never quite understand. I suppose that when it came to doing what needed to be done, she could potentially overlook anything.

I watched. Then I noticed that Mr Rivers was no longer alone. A boy had approached – from where I knew not – and had begun to untangle the horse's reins from the post. Mr Rivers stood motionless as the boy carefully worked, the boy's hesitancy revealing an evident preoccupation with error. He had the bearing of a student under the watch of an abusive schoolmaster, unsure of himself, and braced for a strike. Mr Rivers remained still as the boy continued, and not once did this boy look up at his employer. The boy was afraid, even after he had managed to release the reins, and Mr Rivers, it was clear, meant to do nothing to provide him comfort.

And then I noticed something else as I peered more intently through the lace. The boy was a boy I knew – or at least a boy I was almost certain I knew. As Mr Rivers mounted the horse, and the boy turned just enough for me to see his face, I recognised, below the sagging cap, that very same boy who had delivered the letter informing me of Mr Luckhurst's death. Yes – I was sure of it. The messenger boy, the bearer of the wretched news that set us on this course. My throat closed for a moment, and the air in the room grew thick, and though the sun was bursting in the sky above, shadows puddled the ground. In my uncertainty I parted the curtain to confirm my suspicion, not thinking that I might not remain undiscovered. But Mr Rivers, responding as plainly as if I had called to him, glanced up towards the window, tipped his hat, and rode off.

That night, it was to begin.

John had been energised by the visit from Mr Rivers, despite mother's comments during dinner that we should, at least initially, 'proceed with caution'. I do not mean to imply that at the time mother was not charmed by Mr Rivers, because she was, but her habit was to question fortune, regardless of how warranted it might seem. John continued to hail Mr Rivers's admirable qualities – his business acumen, his devotion to the trade, his attention to the details that we never could have retained ourselves. Mr Rivers, as mother first suggested, did indeed seem like some kind of remuneration, despite his questionable background. What remained shocking was that such an 'asset' as himself had gone undetected by us for so long.

John and I spent our usual evening in the drawing room, and when the hour turned late, we said goodnight, and John withdrew to his room with Mr Jayne. I remained in the drawing room for another hour or so, reading, and gave Susan permission to retire. I remember I was reading an instalment of the last book by Mr Dickens, who had died earlier that year, and whose new works I would surely miss. The fire was simmering down, and the glow on my lamp was low, and the shadows from the dying flames were creeping irregularly across the wall. The paper in that room held shapes as irregular as shadows. Though the colours were brilliant – bright blues and greens, with a hint of gold – that pattern was one that melted in different directions, depending on the light.

I fell asleep – for how long I cannot say – but the room was dark, save for the orange glow of the embers, when I was awakened by a horrible cry. At first I thought the cry must have come from my own dreaming. I shifted, and a coal in the fire whispered as it crumbled. I was awake, and no sooner had I opened my eyes when I heard the cry again.

It was John.

I turned up the lamp and rushed down the hall to his room.

'John?' I called.

But no answer came. I heard nothing. I called his name again, and when there was still no sound, I tried the handle.

The door was locked.

'John?' I called again, and again there was silence. I of course had the other key, but it was in my own room upstairs. I raced up and returned, and fumbled to get the key into the lock. The key rattled, and through that noise I swear I heard John, in the faintest voice, cry:

'Leave me.'

I threw open the door, and before me was a scene of wretchedness that froze me in my steps. John was curled up, in one corner of his great bed, his hair torn wild, the sheets tangled about him like shrouds, his eyes white and glazed by the bright light of his lamp.

'John!' I said rushing to him. 'John, what is it?'

His hair was soaked through, as if he had been suffering for some time. And now his mouth was open – stuck, frozen – though no sound was coming out of it. He was staring at the wall – at the green curves beyond his bed. The light from his bedside in that dark room was casting contortions of every kind.

I looked where he was looking. Nothing there – only the wall.

John was breathing heavily, and I sat beside him and held him. The sheets were all twisted, and I pulled them from his shoulders. I touched the side of his cheek. He was clammy and warm.

'A nightmare,' I said. 'You may just have had a nightmare.'

He blinked. His eyes were wet with tears that did not fall.

'No,' he said, and his breathing increased again, but I continued to hold him.

I waited. John held me, and his grip was strong. I observed his face, and the pattern of his breath, and slowly both continued to soften. His forehead was damp. I brushed the hair from his face. He leaned back into the headboard and after some time, at last, relaxed.

'A nightmare,' he finally said.

'What was it?' I asked.

He peered at the wall again.

'I don't know,' he said.

And then he looked down.

'I cannot say.'

He had made a kind of fortress from the sheets and the other bedclothes, and he began to move these away in an attempt to release himself from the muddle.

My heart had been racing but it started to calm. John was not prone to nightmares. John had suffered every sort of imaginable illness, but the soundness of his sleep was one thing we had always been thankful for. My first thought of apprehension was that perhaps some new affliction was coming upon him – something that he had managed to elude, until now.

'Shall I stay with you?' I said.

John shook his head. His expression was very dark, and his gaze was fixed on the foot of his bed.

I moved to rise.

'Lucy,' he said, grasping me. 'I must ask you something that I have never asked you before.'

Even today, I tremble at the voice of that memory. And I can never forget my brother's face in that awful moment before he asked. Before he unsealed the covenant that had long protected us from so much.

I squeezed his hand.

'The night that he died . . .' John began.

But then he stopped. The shadows were now playing upon him – shades and dark outlines screwing themselves up across his bed.

'That night . . .' John went on, 'did you see what he saw?'

The shock of the question petrified me. I was so unprepared. Indeed, nothing that had transpired during the ten years since we had lost Tom could ever have prepared me for such a question. Oh, Tom – Tom! No one could see what you saw. And yet, whether from selfish curiosity or fever-ish desire, that is what anyone would have wanted most: to have been able to have seen what you saw. To know. That is, if they could have stood the horror of it.

I had to be careful with how I answered this question. John was returning, and I did not want him to fall back.

'John—' I began.

But he gripped me again, and exclaimed:

'You were there with him, in the room. You – the only one!'

So yes, here we were at last. He was wanting to know if I had seen it. Wanting to know what I knew.

I saw Tom staring at his wall – at the shapes, at his paper. At the intricate design that had entertained us as children. But that was all – I couldn't see anything more then. They did not yet want me to see.

'John,' I repeated. 'Tom saw what he saw. I cannot pre-tend to fully comprehend what took him.'

What took him. And now I think that if I *had* been able to see, and been able to listen, I might have taken Tom from the house. I might have saved him.

John released his grip on me, and I released mine, and his face softened more and was quieted. I should have known to have taken him away then, too, but I didn't. Instead, I fixed his sheets for him, made sure the window was fastened, and ordered my brother back to sleep.

V

THE NEXT DAY we received another visit from Mr Rivers, who said that his plans had changed and that he would be returning to Devon on the train that evening.

'Leaving us so soon,' mother said. 'Such a pity. We haven't yet had the opportunity for you to come and dine.'

She had readied herself in a better dress this time, and I was pleased.

'Thank you, Mrs Braithwhite,' Mr Rivers replied. 'There will be ample opportunities. I expect to be in London much more now, in my new position.'

'In London more – that's good,' mother said. 'And again, we can't thank you enough. Though we were generally aware of Mr Luckhurst's comings and goings, he would often surprise us, which was lovely, but the longer stretches without him left us . . . wanting. I suppose it will be the same with you?'

Mr Rivers smiled.

'You will see me often,' he said. 'The company is entering a new era, and Mr Braithwhite will need to stay apprised.'

John nodded in appreciation. There were no traces of the previous night's episode upon him. His look was bright and his face was clear. Mr Rivers, it seemed, was very good for him.

'Any idea when you will be back then, Rivers?' John said.

'Two weeks,' Mr Rivers replied. 'There is a problem with one of the mine shafts. Some of the machinery is failing. It is best that I oversee the matter myself, given the . . . delicacy.'

He glanced at me, then at mother, who would have taken the point more personally. I was right, for by the sudden and slight projection of her chin, I could see that she had perceived his suggestion. By 'delicacy' he meant 'accident' – the fabled accident that had occurred down in Devon nearly twenty years ago.

I watched mother, expecting her lip to quiver, but she remained firm and said nothing.

'Quite right, Rivers,' John said. 'You go down and see to it. No one better, certainly, and you just send word if you need approvals.'

'Of course, sir,' Mr Rivers replied.

Mother then began fidgeting.

'Mr Rivers,' I interjected, 'is it your understanding that the mining operations are . . . strong?'

Mr Rivers turned towards me.

'Very strong,' he replied. 'The mines have never been stronger. And we've been yielding three, sometimes four times the amount of copper that we predicted at the onset of the year. So I'd say they're beyond strong, Miss Braithwhite, which gives me great confidence. The yields from the mines, together with the increase in the demand for papers, are preparing Braithwhite & Company for triumph into the next century.'

Mother relaxed slightly, and smiled with difficulty.

'Thank you,' she said.

'And I can only repeat,' Mr Rivers went on, 'that my deepest concerns lie not just with the company, but with this family. The reputation of Braithwhite & Company is something I hold in higher esteem than my own, and there is nothing I wouldn't do to protect it. My predecessor saw himself not simply as the manager but as the guardian of the company, and during our many years together, he instilled that deeper sense of duty in me as well. And so, rest assured that whether I am in London or in Devon, or anywhere else in the world, your interests will always be foremost, and right here, before me.'

He was gallant – it was hard to see anything else. And of course these reassuring remarks were another allusion to the long-ago incident, as reputation and esteem had been precisely what the accident in Devon had compromised. I had no doubt that the safeguarding of reputation had been part of Mr Rivers's training, and that he understood that the importance of reputation could not be overestimated. The conversation, the careful handling of his words to mother and to all of us, gave me great insight into the way he manoeuvred. There would never be an open or direct conversation about that past event with him – no reference to the families who had lost their children, or the things the company had done to keep all of that sordid business out of the London papers. Mr Rivers, like that other beloved figure Mr L, would instead be our silent advocate in all matters.

Mr Rivers left us, and that evening, I imagined him on the train to Devon, snaking his way through the goyles and plains of grass. The last red streaks of the day would be fading away in the west during his journey, and night would be comfortably settling in with its faint stars gleaming in a violet sky. Oh – to be with him on that incredible journey! My last time on it had been ten years ago, when I was fourteen – just before Tom died. Tom was with us then, and in his young eyes were the reflections of the tints and patterns of the moorland – the mounds of stolid heather, the gentler wisps of white-seeded grass, paler and darker greens and browns, and the unbending phalanxes of swamp rushes. All of it beautifully mingled with the grey of the rocks and the blue of the streams. All of it changing before our very eyes as shadows fleeted over the broad horizon.

How I longed for it. How knowing he was going there made me think of my little brother, and want so much to see again all that I often missed.

But wasn't it strange? One of the most puzzling aspects about the appearance of Mr Rivers had to do with how his arrival had somehow excited, or revived rather, so many things. I wondered if he too experienced these feelings. Being from the west country, he must have spent his own time roaming the hills and valleys, though I knew nothing of his childhood, or whether it might have permitted such a thing. But I imagined him – a younger Julian Rivers out there with us, taking in sights so vast and beautiful as to consume us like the dark waters of the bogs themselves. Had Mr Rivers, like us, been terrified of the legend of the escaped convict – a French prisoner whose ghost wandered the moors in search of badly behaved children? If he found you, it was said, he would take you to his lair, where he would cut out your heart and roast it with onions, before disposing of the rest of you in the bog. Or had Mr Rivers, in his youth, ever visited the 'six children' – the cluster of rocks shaped like tombstones that John and Tom and I had discovered in a hidden valley? The rocks stood there in a misshapen circle, some as small as Tom, others as tall as John – a family of hungry orphans, waiting to be claimed.

There was endless discovery; the patterns were always changing. And that last year that we had Tom, he said something very strange. We were, the three of us, sitting on our own stones near the six children, when Tom, with no provocation whispered out:

'I should grieve to go away and think that anyone was glad that I was gone, or didn't care.'

John and I remained silent for a moment, and John, who had been tossing about some rocks between his feet, sat up and threw one into the distance.

'Why should you think no one would care?' I said.

Tom looked at me with sad eyes.

'Did anyone care for these children?' he said.

'I don't know, Tom,' I replied. 'We don't know who they were. But if they were indeed ever children, then somebody must have cared for them.'

This was Tom, melancholy Tom, who sensed more than any of us that time was a horrible thief. His thoughts were like a swift and rapid river, which he felt forced to try and stop, but could not. His childish hands were incapable of damming up anything, and so that river flowed within him, moving him, rushing him, until he would at last cry out. And I heard him. I was his comfort – sometimes, I thought, his only comfort – because he said so many things that nobody wanted to hear. Tom's small, beautiful thoughts mirrored the shadowy land itself, half silver in the moonlight, but also half gloom.

He was there, down in Devon, where we no longer visited. He was down there where Mr Rivers was going, without me.

Mr Rivers was gone, as he said, for about two weeks, until the first chilly days of October. In the interim we received many notes of consolation on the death of Mr Luckhurst, and many requests for calls, most of which we refused. The truth is, we had stopped receiving regular calls some years before. With John's health steadily uncertain, and mother's continued inclination towards isolation, our leanings towards welcoming visitors had all but evaporated. And this suited because the unforgiving curiosity about the company had already started, and the gossip about town was . . . well, how shall I put it? Unfriendly.

In any case, most of the visitors had stopped, one of the few exceptions being Mr and Mrs Stapleton-Grace, who lived in a dishevelled family house near Regent's Park. What to say about them? I never terribly liked them, and mother didn't either, but they were from such a good family that father hadn't been able to resist befriending them, and so for years they had been coming around. Yes, our association with them went back as far as that, back to the earliest days of father having inherited the company. The Stapleton-Graces had no money, but that hadn't concerned father, the more important thing being Mr Stapleton-Grace's various connections. The thing that perturbed me, though, when I was finally old enough to comprehend it, was that there was a predatory streak about them, even though they were the ones whom people fawned over.

But they were nice people (they had been genuinely kind to mother after father's death, and again after Tom's), and they paid us a visit that first week, during Mr Rivers's absence. John, thank goodness, had experienced no more wretched nights since that first, and he was feeling quite well, and was thus in the drawing room with us when they came.

'I say, John, you really are looking alive,' Mr Stapleton-Grace began. 'It's been ages since we've seen you, and we're very glad to see you today.'

'Yes,' Mrs Stapleton-Grace added, 'very glad.'

John smiled with appreciation. I poured out the tea.

'An awful turn, about Luckhurst,' Mr Stapleton-Grace said. 'Awful for the company. Awful for the family. But John, it seems you may at last be up for filling the role? It's a vast empire to handle, but perhaps the time has come.'

John managed a lesser smile. Mr Stapleton-Grace could be so indelicate. He was no stranger to the unpredictability of John's condition, and knew very well why in all these years John had never taken his proper place at the company.

John was about to respond when mother interrupted:

'We've found the most delightful manager – one of the office men from Devon.'

Mr Stapleton-Grace made a show of surprise.

'Ah . . .' he said.

'Already?' Mrs Stapleton-Grace asked.

'He's quite delightful,' mother said, her cheeks colouring. 'And has apparently been with us for some time.

He has been under Mr Luckhurst's tutelage going back many years now.'

'Julian Rivers,' John said.

Mr Stapleton-Grace thought for a moment.

'Never heard of him,' he said.

'No,' John said, 'we hadn't either. But it just goes to show you how Mr Luckhurst was always thinking.'

'That certainly seems fortunate,' Mrs Stapleton-Grace added.

'It's more than fortunate,' John said. 'The man is quite brilliant. Not only does he understand the old ways of the company, but is full of new ideas as well. He is precisely what Braithwhite & Company needs to carry itself into the next century.'

And to close the matter, mother said:

'Precisely.'

Mr and Mrs Stapleton-Grace were not the types who ever showed any sort of contrition, and they stirred their tea and moved on to the next topic, while mother patiently answered their questions and maintained her posture. The visit continued, and at last the tea was gone, and neither mother nor I called Susan to bring up more. Our guests' movement towards departure remained behind the usual silences, until at last mother offered:

'It was so good of you to come.'

The Stapleton-Graces nodded and smiled, and Mrs Stapleton-Grace smoothed her plentiful skirts.

'There was one more thing,' Mr Stapleton-Grace said, 'that I wanted to mention, before we take our leave of you.'

I knew it was coming – it always did. I just didn't know what it would be.

'Please,' mother replied.

Her hands were lightly clasped together on her lap, and she remained upright and attentive, in anticipation of what she hoped would be a final point to this visit.

Mr Stapleton-Grace reached into one of his coat pockets and pulled out a piece of paper.

'Have you . . .' he hesitated. 'Have you seen the article in today's *Reader*?'

Mother's mouth moved, and her eyes narrowed on him.

'What article?' she said.

Mrs Stapleton-Grace again moved her hands over her skirts.

'Oh, it's nothing to be alarmed about, Clarissa,' she said. 'It's just another notice with—'

She paused.

'Yes?' mother said.

'Well,' Mrs Stapleton-Grace said, 'it has implications.'

'What kind of implications?' mother said.

'Nothing direct,' Mr Stapleton-Grace said. 'They continue with their nonsense. We just thought you should be aware.'

He reached his hand out towards mother, offering her the piece of paper, which by now I could see was a small clipping from that morning's *London Reader*. Mother motioned with her hand to pass the paper instead to John, which Mr Stapleton-Grace did, quite awkwardly.

John looked down at the paper.

'Well?' mother said. 'What is it?'

I already knew what it was. Another wretched piece of 'reporting' – or at least what at the time I could only think of as wretched.

John was perusing.

'Well?' mother repeated.

'It's another notice about the arsenic,' I said.

Every eye, except John's, turned to look at me. Then Mrs Stapleton-Grace turned to mother.

'Nothing severe is mentioned,' she said.

'No,' Mr Stapleton-Grace agreed, 'but the fools do make their implications.'

Mother stiffened, and I was starting to grow hot. The Stapleton-Graces should have known better.

A moment passed, and John finally breathed.

'Well, John?' mother said.

My brother looked up.

'It's a small thing,' he said.

'Very small,' Mrs Stapleton-Grace confirmed.

'But an annoyance just the same,' Mr Stapleton-Grace added.

'Do read it,' mother said.

I was angry. I am ashamed to say it, but in that moment I could only feel anger. The Stapleton-Graces were supposedly mother's friends, and yet time and time again they did all sorts of things that only caused her more worry.

John looked down, and began to read.

ARSENIC IN WALL-PAPERS

FREQUENT *protests have been made by medical men and others interested in the health of the community, against the extensive use of wall-papers which are being coloured by preparations containing arsenic. In the green papers especially, arsenic is present to an*

*injurious degree; and where such papers cover the walls
of sitting-rooms, and more particularly bed-rooms, the
health of the inmates is often known materially to suf-
fer.*

*Of fifty samples of wall-paper lately examined by
Professor P. S. Kenley, more than half were found to
contain arsenic. The arsenic was present either as arsenite of copper or aceto-arsenite of copper. Two samples,
not reported, which contained extensive green colour,
were found to contain arsenic; and several papers with
green figures upon them contained heavy amounts of
the same material.*

*It is reasonable to assume that to the presence of
such deleterious ingredients in wall-papers we may
ascribe many little illnesses of children where no
apparent cause exists, and which sometimes puzzle the
medical attendant.*

Mother put a hand to her forehead. Her hand trembled.
One of her headaches was coming on.

'More nonsense,' Mr Stapleton-Grace said.

'Yes,' John said. 'The doctors have all gone mad.'

It was exactly what our father would have said, if he had
been there.

'I cannot . . .' mother said.

'It's just that with Mr Luckhurst now gone . . .' Mrs
Stapleton-Grace said.

'We need not be reminded that Mr Luckhurst is gone,'
mother whispered.

The room fell silent. I resented them for bringing this
pernicious influence in, though they were the only ones I
could find fault with at the time. In that moment, I knew

nothing more than that I needed to get mother away from them – quickly, or there would be consequences.

'We appreciate the—' I began.

But Mr Stapleton-Grace interrupted.

'Another child has died,' he said. 'About ten years old. Unfortunate thing. Had been complaining for some time about pains in her limbs and back. Pale and fretful.'

'Sounds like spinal fever,' John said.

His annoyance was very plain.

'It does,' Mr Stapleton-Grace said. 'But they could not come to any conclusions. They called a council of homeo-pathic doctors, who finally diagnosed rheumatism of the heart. But she was sick only another day when she died.'

'And in her room, she had . . .' Mrs Stapleton-Grace managed.

But thankfully, she stopped herself.

'Mother,' I said, 'I think we must get you to your room.'

I then stared straight into the eyes of Mr Stapleton-Grace, and for the briefest moment, he started. I imagined him dead, locked up and rotting in a box somewhere, an ironic victim of his own obsession with these poisons.

And yes, I do realise it was very unkind of me to do so. But I couldn't help it. They always seemed to be backing us into a corner like this.

'Thank you, I'm sorry,' Mr Stapleton-Grace said to the room. 'Eugenia, come, we must leave these lovely Braithwhites. John, again, I am thrilled to see you looking so good.'

We all stood, and Mrs Stapleton-Grace kissed mother. We then rang for Mr Jayne, who escorted our guests downstairs.

I took mother up to her room, settled her comfortably into her chair, and after a while returned to the drawing room, where John was looking over some papers. He had been involving himself in company matters more deeply, and his revival had changed the whole feeling in our house. I did not want anything to compromise that revival, and I was hoping – and assuming – that he could dismiss these most recent irritations. Had the Stapleton-Graces been trying to help us in some way? The answer is unclear to me, even to this day. What's more important is that the scent of the whole thing was finally coming up. It was everywhere, even though none of us could smell it.

'Can you imagine,' John said to me after a bit, 'what father would think if he were ever forced to listen to such nonsense? Wallpaper killing children. Our beautiful, beautiful wallpaper. The doctors have all gone mad. Next thing you know, they'll be telling you to get rid of all your hats and dinner gowns because they contain too much arsenic.'

But at the moment I was not much concerned with all that. I was rather still angry at myself for not stopping the conversation before mother had become so upset.

'What people say amongst themselves is bad enough,' I said, 'without the Stapleton-Graces bringing it in here.'

'They always manage to do it somehow.'

'Yes, I know. It's remarkable.'

John continued to move his papers. There were many of them scattered across the table.

'Madness,' he said at last.

And that ended it for the evening.

My brother was so handsome, and his profile against the blue and green swirls on the walls augmented the stateliness of the drawing room's contours. Our beautiful drawing room. Our beautiful paper. As beautiful as anyone was willing to see. The sun shone in through father's lofty windows, and all was bright, though all was not glowing. I can see that now, when I think back on that room – that the glow was perpetually in a state of fading. Something about that state was what forced me to stay on guard, for while the sun shone in, and no matter how extraordinary the reflections, there was something else – a darkness – that we would never be able to keep out.

VI

I REMEMBER MR Luckhurst once returning from a botanical expedition to the tropics, and telling us of a great kind of storm that occurs there – a hurricane – which grows in ferocity as it forms over the ocean's warm waters, and destroys whole islands within minutes. At the centre of these storms is something called an 'eye' – a small circle of total peace and calm, around which the ravaging monster rotates. One could stand single-footed in the eye, Mr Luckhurst said, and balance a straw upon one's nose without the least consequence, while all around you the horrendous storm devastates everything in its path. I did not know it at the time, but we were in our 'eye' – a disquieting place of serenity where John had shed nearly every sign of previous illness. It is remarkable how quickly we can grow comfortable with the good, when the bad that we resent has retreated for only a short while. I say this not because I was ever resentful of John's weaknesses, but rather to chastise myself for thinking that any respite from what chased us could last.

John was bright. He was cheerful. And I do not think it was simply because of some physiological change in him. I was not privy to the contents of the letters that arrived every other day from Mr Rivers, but whatever they might have contained, they had a great effect upon my brother. For those two weeks that Mr Rivers was gone, John revived immeasurably, as he involved himself more in the business, and devoured the various correspondences from the west. Mr Rivers, John told me, had got the mining situation under control right away, and could have come back to London earlier, but thought it best to stay on longer so as to guarantee that everything was right. He was extraordinary. He had an almost preternatural ability to identify the areas of greatest need. It was a shocking thing that this 'man from nowhere', as John jestingly called him, could understand the company – and our family – so well as to have become so quickly inextricable from both.

'He speaks beautifully,' mother commented at dinner one evening, 'though there is something of the country about his vowels.'

I reminded her that Mr Rivers, after all, had come from Morwellham.

'Yes,' she said dimly, 'I wonder . . .'

And she looked off.

'Wonder what, mother?' John said.

Mother continued looking, but not at us.

'He would have been a boy of about ten, I think – when it happened.'

'When what happened?' John said.

Mother was silent for a moment. I could see where she was going. She was never inclined to talk about it. But here it came.

'The accident,' she finally said. 'You were eight, so he must have been about ten.'

Susan and Mr Jayne entered to clear the plates. That gave me some relief. We did not need mother 'wondering' about anything, especially now.

But once the plates were cleared, she resumed.

'A boy of about ten.'

'And?' John said. 'What is the significance of that?'

Mother looked at both of us, as if there were something great that we should already know.

'Well,' she said, 'he would remember it.'

'I've had a letter from him this morning,' John said, turning us away from the whole thing, 'and you will both be happy to hear that the yields on the copper for the past few weeks have been six times the initial estimates. More export for smelting. More material for our formulas. It is capital – capital! Even father could never have foreseen such abundance.'

'Yes he could have,' mother said sharply. 'There was nothing your father couldn't foresee.'

John swallowed.

'Mother,' he said, 'what *is* the matter? Are you all right?'

'I'm sorry,' she said.

Her mind had grown active, and I could always tell when things were 'mounting'. What I now realise – and I am so ashamed to say that I did not see it then – was that the awful visit from the Stapleton-Graces had caused her to check, if temporarily, her growing fondness for Mr Rivers. If, that is, one could actually have called it fondness.

'I have started to wonder just how he is doing it,' she said.

'Doing what?' John said.

'Everything,' mother replied.

'Well, the same way we have always done it.'

'No – there is something different,' mother said. 'The workers . . . what of the workers? Has he said anything about them?'

'No,' John said. 'And why should he?'

'Because they are the barometer. They have always been the barometer. For what we are doing.'

'I am sure the workers are fine, mother,' John said. 'Mr Rivers rushed down to Devon to see about the mines. He fixed what needed to be fixed. That is what he does, and he's marvellous. And while he is fixing things, he has everyone's interests at heart.'

'Yes,' mother said, 'but—'

We both looked at her. Her face was not worried, but rather firm.

'Does he *have* a heart?' she said.

John set down his fork and knife. One could see that he was irritated. And yet unlike father, he would not erupt. My brother had always been much better that way.

'Mother,' he said, though his voice was not all calm. 'I am not sure what you're suggesting. I have never met a more noble, more dedicated, or more conscientious man than Mr Rivers. In this short time he has proven himself to be exactly what this company – *what this family* – has needed for many years now. He is at the top of the heap, mother, and we can afford no less. And as far as the workers go, I do know he's gone about them, and goes about them regularly. He is no stranger to them, or their struggles. He comes from them, after all.'

Mother lowered her chin. She was mistrustful by nature. And yet that mistrust conflicted with how much she understood that we wanted Mr Rivers – needed him – in our lives. She never could handle these kinds of conflicts very well though, and she was showing signs that the conversation had become too much for her.

62

'Shall we go up, mother?' I said.

Mother grimaced.

'Yes, I think that would be best.'

Susan came in then to finish clearing the table, and mother and I left John to himself in the dining room. Upstairs, mother was shaken, and the headache had come on, just as I had feared. Some moments passed, and Susan soon arrived, but I sent her back down to fetch some warm water. Mother's eyes had begun darting about the room. In her chamber, another one of our aviary patterns covered the walls with a horrible flock of birds.

Susan returned.

'Anything else, miss?' she said.

'Thank you, no,' I said, and dismissed her.

Then I got mother into bed, and placed a warm compress over her eyes. The compresses were the only things that ever soothed her.

'All right, mother?' I said.

Mother breathed out a few times.

'Yes . . . yes . . .' she said.

She was drifting – or trying to.

I sat there with her near the bed. She would not be able to fall asleep right away. The headache would last for some time, even if it were one of the mild ones.

Mother breathed.

'It is getting more dreadful,' she said at last.

I did not reply. Mother remained quiet and I turned down the lamp. The eyes of all the birds on the walls glistened in the shadows. There were green birds and blue birds and yellow and blue – a swarm of Henry's wretched cousins from remote and exotic places.

I watched mother breathe. Something was happening – but not something visible. I could not tell when it had started, but there had been another 'turn'. Ever since Tom, there had been many turns with mother, each one more severe than the one that had come before. John and I were forever on the lookout. We watched for them, and could spot them in a moment. And then the rebound would happen, and all would be well again. This was mother's pattern, the thing that reliably outlined her whole being. But she was older now, and we could no longer take the rebounds for granted.

Was I overreacting to that horrendous visit with the Stapleton-Graces? Had I been too sceptical of what most would have considered signs of genuine friendship and concern? No, because the Stapleton-Graces didn't understand us. No one understood us. And no one would ever be able to truly understand the things we experienced in our own house.

'How is she?' John asked when I met him again later in the drawing room.

'She is sleeping,' I said. 'She was mumbling again before she fell asleep. Nothing coherent. Just her struggles against the headache.'

'You're so good to her, Lucy,' John said. 'And me.'

He had changed. He had been strong at dinner, but now he was somewhat diminished.

'They are getting worse,' I told him. 'She said so.'

John sighed.

'Well, at least she's telling us. Better that than to have her keeping everything to herself.'

The lamplight played upon the walls, and John's face was contemplative. Over the years, amongst many other arts, I had made an art of learning to read him. Like mother, John went so frequently in and out of his various states that gaining *some* mastery over inconsistency was the only way I could do what I needed to do.

We were quiet for a while, and then I moved forward.

'Mr Rivers should return in the next few days,' I said.

John brightened.

'Yes,' he said. 'I look forward to receiving him.'

'It seems that he puts you at great ease,' I said. 'In a way that Mr Luckhurst never really did.'

John looked at me. There was a gleam there, but it was distant.

'You are observant, Lucy,' John said. 'Mr Rivers has become . . .'

And he raised one of his hands to his forehead.

'He has become something quite extraordinary,' he said.

Then he added:

'To me. To us.'

Henry was preening himself – good and beautiful Henry. I could not help but smile, even as worried as I was about mother. John had revived so much in recent weeks.

'He is extraordinary,' I said. 'We've been lucky.'

'Yes,' John said. 'Lucky.'

But there was a darkness to John too. He was not by any means pure excitement. I did not need to ask him anything to know why. You see, John could not quite accept the wonderfulness of Mr Rivers, because Mr Rivers was too great a reflection of what John might have been. By all accounts, John was not supposed to have lived. But he had

65

defied the doctors and everything else for all these years. He had lived. He had crawled out of whatever dark caverns they had condemned him to. And now, with the entrance of this entrancing, wonderful man, who seemed destined to be friend and saviour to us all, no matter the circumstance, we were forced to meet also, face to face, something much more sinister: the unrelenting, unforgiving form of John's demon.

'I remember being in the office in Tavistock once, with father,' John said. 'I was perhaps seven. One of the workers had come in with one of his boys, not much older than I, to ask for an audience. The worker's wife and other child had grown very sick with some sort of lesions that the town doctor could not seem to cure. The man himself did not look well, and the long and the short of it was that he needed money. He was, I think if I am remembering correctly, one of the calciner operators, and his wife was a bal maiden – a riddler or some such. Father was that day sympathetic, as you know he sometimes could be, and agreed to advance the man some wages.'

'Yes,' I said. 'Mother had often spoken of the need for better protective clothing. All sorts of things were always coming about with the workers.'

'But that is not my point here, Lucy,' John said. 'My point has to do with the way father *executed* the agreement. He drew me close to let me observe him count out this man's wages. Very carefully, coin by coin, I watched him in his deliberateness. Once he had the sum piled up, he raised the money into his fingers and dropped it into my hands. 'Now you'll see, John,' he said, 'how powerful a thing money is, and how anxious everyone is to get it. Mr Verris here comes

66

all the way to the office to ask for money, and you, who have the money, are going to give it to him as a great favour.' Then he turned me around to face this Mr Verris, and I deposited the money into the man's hands, rough and dirty as they were.'

John was dark. There, on his face, was the shadow of our father.

'What I cannot forget,' John went on, 'is that boy.'

'I can imagine it must not have been pleasant,' I said, 'knowing father, and the tone he could sometimes set.'

'That boy,' John said, 'the way he looked at me, as I was handing the money over to his father. The details of the dirty face are lost upon me, but what has stayed with me is the glare, which was full of such resentment, such . . .'

A flicker from one of the candles I had brought in made a strange shape on the wall.

'Such, well . . .' John went on, 'with such detestation. That was not the first time I had seen such a look, surely. But it was the first time I had seen it from another boy.'

'I would not have had you in the office that day,' I said. 'In fact, I don't know that I would have had you in the office at all, at that age.'

John shifted in his chair.

'Well,' he said, 'never too early for father.'

Father had not lived to see the progression of John's condition. That was another thing that preoccupied John, and though we never spoke of it, the curse of his 'softness' was always upon him, and was something of which he remained greatly ashamed.

'I was supposed to want to do it,' he said, 'but I'm not sure I ever could have.'

'It happened the way it happened,' I said. 'And we have managed to endure.'

John looked at me, his eyes resplendent amidst the colourful reflections of our drawing room.

'It was impossible from the beginning,' he said. 'But we're going into our next phase, and we are not alone.'

Then he almost gasped.

'Thank goodness for Mr Rivers.'

No matter what happened, there would never be any distance between me and John.

'Yes,' I said. 'Thank goodness for him.'

VII

IN A FEW days' time, I decided that I should do something out of the ordinary. The chill of the first days of October, to which I referred earlier, had already set in, and the city had taken on that hurried change in motion that normally precedes winter. We anticipated Mr Rivers's return to London any day now, and John had been occupied preparing various business items for discussion. It seemed a fine day to leave him, as he had got a very good and early start. And mother, too, appeared quite together at breakfast, having had a sound night's sleep with no disturbances and no headaches.

Susan accompanied me, and we left Marylebone and walked ourselves south towards Oxford Street. It had been quite some time since I had been out. The air was crisp – clear – and the sky was blue. A wonderful day to walk, and a rare day to be unencumbered by wet skirts and umbrellas. We hastened along Harley Street, speedily moving past all the doctors that father had not been fond of, through Cavendish Square – a lovely square, truly – and then on to Regent Street where the crowd thickened and moved in both directions. We joined in the river-flow of people on that great avenue and wound our way all the way down to the onerous Strand. We were not too long in getting there, as I never allowed us to slow our pace.

When walking, I often found it best to get out of our neighbourhood as quickly as possible.

The Strand was as noisy and irksome as I always remembered, and there, perfectly perched not far from the turn to Waterloo Bridge, was the stout, six-storey stone ancestor that held the showrooms and offices of Braithwhite & Company. Father's offices – the family's offices. The windows were rotating exhibits of art, displaying that season's choicest selections in an explosion of pattern and colour. When I was a child, standing in front of these windows made me dizzy. The colours and shapes and distortions and creatures were all too much for me, as they had been at home. Child or no, one – or at least I – had to be careful with Braithwhite papers. Their designs were so beguiling and their colours so alluring that one never knew where the mind would wander, if one stared for too long.

Inside, on the ground floor, was the main showroom, which we would need to travel through to reach the steps to the offices upstairs. Again, it had been quite some time since I had been here – years I think – but the smell of it was the same, and the walls were as magnificent as ever. I say magnificent in the 'enormous' sense, because there was so much to take in that it was difficult to comprehend all at once. One of my favourite observations left over from when I was younger, was seeing the crowds of unsuspecting gawkers as they steered themselves through our displays. All around on the various walls were papers that most perceived as lush and beautiful, ready to transform any drawing room, bedroom, dining room, or library. In the sample books, which rested like great pieces of granite on the counters, you could turn the thick pages to discover endless selections of patterns, each specimen more intricate in conception, more original in style than the one you had previously eyed. I stopped to look into one of the pattern books myself, and found the most astonishingly coloured samples I had ever seen – bright and dizzying. My head swooned a bit at the boldness of the colours, and the extravagant, reckless motions of the designs.

A memory flooded in upon me – that of the day, when I was a young girl, and had accompanied father and John out to one of the factories in Chiswick. There was all manner of printing activity going on in the factory, with so many men applying paint to large pattern blocks, and then stamping the coated blocks onto the endless reams of paper. But what I remember most about that day was the man who was mixing the colours. He was off to one side of the printing room, separate from the others, surrounded by buckets of pigment and chalk. He was pouring a great stream of dark green paint from a small pail into a larger bucket as we passed him. John and father walked on, but I stopped, unnoticed. The man remained undisturbed by my watching him.

The man set down the pail and began stirring the poured pigment into the chalk. As the two ingredients mixed, the colour became brighter, and the whole of the substance transformed into the most brilliant shade of green. The man gripped the outer edge of the bucket as, with a wooden paddle, he stirred, and on one of his knuckles, which protruded like a rock under his skin, I noticed a rather large sore.

That sore – the bright red ruby shimmering above the liquid emerald. That is what I most remember – the alarming colour of that sore. The man stirred. The sore was dried and flaked around the edges, but in the centre the sore glistened as the man held onto the bucket. Would the awful thing burst, I wondered? Would it bleed into the mixture? Would it contaminate that singular colour with a droplet from something so awful?

The man observed me, and he stopped. I felt caught – wrong to have been staring.

The man looked down at me, then at his hand, and then back at me again.

One must take care, Miss Braithwhite, he said.

Then I heard father up ahead, shouting my name.

The man's words came back to me as I flipped the pages of the sample books. *Take care.* Then the words faded, as quickly as the whole memory had returned. Susan and I continued winding our way to the back of the showroom and ascended the staircase. The passage was dark, but we emerged into brightness. I was surprisingly winded by our climb.

Take care.

The room at the top of the staircase was as busy as I remembered – busier perhaps – with men at long tables tabulating and annotating and scribbling. Different in tone from the fantastical room below, the office held a simpler paper – a blue, brown and white pattern of repeating arches and fronds, as orderly and as regular as the men who filled the space. And at the centre of the office, though much more towards the front of the building, was the great glass chamber, raised on a dais, that Mr Luckhurst – and before him, our father – had occupied.

When Susan and I appeared at the head of the steps, Mr Ismay, one of the managers whom I had known since I was small, looked up with delight and rushed over to us.

'Miss Braithwhite!' he exclaimed. 'It has been forever since we've seen you. Welcome back to the house. And you're looking very well, under the circumstances, if you'll forgive me. I am deeply sorry about what's happened. It struck us all very hard.'

'Thank you, Mr Ismay,' I said. 'You're very kind, and it is wonderful to see you. Susan takes good care of me, and we are all quite fine at the house.'

'That is good. And Mr Braithwhite?'

'My brother is doing well,' I said, 'and even better lately, which of course brings us great relief.'

'I'm delighted,' Mr Ismay replied. 'It truly is a lovely thing to see you. Will you stop for some tea then?'

'Yes, that would be very nice.'

I sent Susan back downstairs to the showroom, while Mr Ismay and I retired to one of the outer offices that, like father's glass workspace, overlooked the entire room. The waiting room – it was a small parlour really – was panelled on all sides, with the remaining wall of windows facing out over the offices. How many times I had run my fingers along those panels, waiting for father to finish parading John through his army of clerks.

Mr Ismay called for tea.

'Really,' Mr Ismay said, 'I am so happy that you've come. Mr Luckhurst was spending so much time down in Devonshire in recent years, that we saw him less, and consequently heard little about how you and your family were getting along. I know that some years ago it was very bad with Mr Braithwhite . . .'

'Yes,' I said. 'Very bad.'

'And—'

'Yes,' I interrupted. 'And mother too. It was looking rather hopeless there for a while. But we've all come out of it now, and things have been looking up.'

'Due in great part, if not entirely, to *your* industry.'

I blushed. Mr Ismay had always been kind.

The tea arrived, and the young man carrying it poured out two cups for us, and then left.

'And may I ask,' I began, 'how things are here? You can imagine that with such a change, we have our concerns.'

'Yes, it is a dramatic thing,' Mr Ismay said, sorrowfully. 'One thinks the day will never come and then it does. But Mr Luckhurst was brilliant, as you know. He put the company before everything else. Unlike many of us, he anticipated – well, everything. We will never have another like him.'

Mr Ismay sipped his tea. I suppose he was being respectful. He was not going to offer up much more.

'Can I ask then,' I continued, 'are you pleased with the new management?'

Mr Ismay looked at me, quizzically.

'Mr Rivers,' I said.

'Ah-ah, yes,' he said. 'Forgive me. He is still somewhat of a stranger to me. And a man of his age . . . well, I have no doubt—'

'He is a stranger to you, Mr Ismay? Has he not been with the company for more than ten years?'

Mr Ismay frowned.

'Ten years? Well, no. I don't think so.'

'But he informed us that he was a veteran member of the company,' I said.

'It's possible,' Mr Ismay replied. 'He comes from the Devon office, so I've met him ever so rarely.'

Mr Ismay set down his tea cup, which clinked on the saucer with a kind of finality.

'But he's frequented London,' I suggested. 'With Mr Luckhurst.'

'He may have. I can only tell you that I haven't much seen him.'

How strange, I thought, that a man like Mr Rivers, who had such obvious and thorough knowledge of all of the company's operations, could be 'rare' to someone as knowledgeable as Mr Ismay.

'But Mr Rivers,' I said, 'will be managing this office as well now, yes?'

'That is what I hear,' Mr Ismay said. 'Though how he will manage the two offices single-handedly I do not know. Ah well, you know, the young . . .'

He was not being serious, and this too surprised me.

'You must forgive me for pressing the point, Mr Ismay, but really I would like to know, for my sake as well as for the sake of my brother, aside from this recent trip to Devon, has Mr Rivers been in attendance here regularly?'

Mr Ismay then did turn serious.

'Well . . .' he hesitated. 'No, miss.'

He was a gentle man who did not like trouble.

'No?' I asked.

'No.'

'Well, how can that be?'

'I don't know, miss.'

This was certainly a very odd thing. My face grew hot.

'But Mr Rivers is running the company, is he not?'

'Please, Miss Braithwhite,' Mr Ismay said. 'I do not want to alarm you. A visit from you is such an uncommon thing. I am only here – at your service.'

'Then be so kind as to tell me how Mr Rivers is running the company if he is never here.'

'Well, miss,' Mr Ismay said, 'we are all running the company. And as you say, I believe he's gone to Devon.'

And then after a pause he added:

'It is not as if he's never here. He is. Just not – dependably.'

It was not impossible to imagine – the company running itself. For as I have described before, the company was a kind of organism, whole unto itself. But at the same time there had always been someone firmly at the helm of it, and this latest information from Mr Ismay was, well, outright bursting my vision. All along, I had been picturing Julian Rivers – this glorious Julian Rivers – manning our family's offices, and overseeing the whole spectacle from father's glass tower. If he weren't regularly here, guaranteeing the company's operations during this time of greatest need, then where was he, and what was he doing?

Mr Ismay, I could see, was noting my concern, and he offered a weak smile as he tried to decide what to say next.

'The most recent returns are extraordinary,' he offered.

'Thank you, Mr Ismay,' I replied. 'We've been informed of that too.'

Clearly he did not want me to ask any more questions. I waited, unsure of how to pursue what I wanted to know. Then Mr Ismay sipped his tea again, and leaned forward.

'You do know, miss . . .'

And he paused.

'Well, I do feel unquestionably terrible saying it, but you do know that Mr Luckhurst's last few years were . . .'

He turned his cup in his saucer.

'They were not great ones.'

'What do you mean?' I asked.

'I admired him,' Mr Ismay said, 'as much as anyone else present, but Mr Luckhurst had, in recent years, missed things. Things had slipped. We were aware.'

'I see,' I said.

'And, well,' Mr Ismay continued, 'we only supposed that the returns were so successful, month after month, and year after year, because of some other kind of backing. And many of us assumed, rightly I think, that that backing might have been coming from Mr Rivers.'

'And why is that?'

'Because Mr Luckhurst was always down in Devon,' Mr Ismay said. 'Even when he didn't need to be.'

He inflected what he was saying with the strangest intonation. There was such complexity to what he was suggesting. Had Mr Luckhurst spent so much time down in Devon because of Mr Rivers, then? Obviously, Mr L had been preparing Mr Rivers to succeed him, in the event that anything should happen. Now something *had* happened, and Mr Rivers had succeeded. And we had never known anything about it, which was the strangest thing of all.

'The operation down there was tight as a lock, miss – still is. They grew very close and, well, as you know, Mr Braithwhite was never here. Mr Luckhurst and Mr Rivers . . . I think they came to depend on each other. Yes, they came to depend on each other a great deal.'

Mr Ismay, to his credit, was being so careful. The company was the company because of men like him.

'The one thing I will say,' he offered, 'is that three years ago, at the Exposition Universelle in Paris, when Braithwhite & Company brought home every prize, it was Mr Rivers's name, and not Mr Luckhurst's, that had been attached to all the submissions.'

I sat upright.

'Mr Rivers?' I said, though not disbelievingly.

Mr Ismay nodded.

'The fact is that Mr Rivers is not the "new management". He is simply the management, as that is what, I surmise, he has been for some years now.'

'But how . . .' I protested, 'how did he come to be the management in the first place? This person whom you, one of our most established managers, claim to barely know?'

Mr Ismay moved his mouth, but did not quite smile.

'Well, miss,' he said, 'I think there must have been some arrangement.'

'What sort of arrangement?' I pressed.

'I don't know,' Mr Ismay replied.

How he couldn't know or why he wouldn't say overwhelmed me, and feeling myself growing ever more desperate, I decided that it would be best for me to go. I thanked Mr Ismay for his kindness and his hospitality, and promised that I would not let so much time pass before I returned. He smiled and took my hands and said that he'd be so glad to see me again, at whatever time I might choose to visit. But despite these cordialities, and the comfort of seeing the office buzzing along as it always had, I was in a much greater state of confusion than I was in when I arrived. Well, confusion is putting it rather mildly. I was worried – about the company, about us. And yet when I thought of Julian Rivers, and the strange gallantry that seemed to surround him, I experienced a fluttery kind of feeling – the thrill one gets when one is truly curious. There was something more here – worse – than curiosity, however. What was it, I wondered. What was it that wasn't right?

Downstairs in the showroom where Susan awaited me, the colours were brilliant and different. I had often been able to find a country haven or two for myself in our papers, but with this new collection, those discoveries had grown impossible. The greens were so bright, and the oranges so fiery that experiencing anything other than being devoured by these colours was beyond one's imaginative reach. The blues swirled like great storms and the pinks and yellows snowed in blizzards. I grew dizzy – yes, yes, it was bound to happen – as the rocks and the feathers all avalanched around me. Susan caught me, just as I was coming off the last step.

'Are you all right, miss?'

'Yes,' I said. 'Of course. Let us be off, Susan. We have more to do, and I think it is time for some air.'

At Covent Garden, the stone pillars greeted us like the columns of a Grecian temple, and inside we would encounter many wonderful and familiar treasures. That would be most welcome after everything I had just heard, and everything I was continuing to turn over in my mind. The market offered what was most exquisite in London – rows upon rows of carrots and parsnips, and green sprouts piled high in cascading pyramids. Apples of all colours, chestnuts in prickly skins, and heaps of quince and persimmon all waiting to be brought home and peeled. Our mission there that day was to collect some squashes and persimmon for Mrs Dawes. She had got it into her mind to do a roast, as well as a pie.

Everyone knew that Mr Thorogood carried the best squashes in the market, so we sought out his stall in the south colonnade, past the tables of cabbages and broccoli. His mounds of squashes dominated the area with their blackish greens, their grey greens, their yellow greens, and light greys. There were squashes of bright yellow, and some that were wrinkled orange, and others that were as smooth and as white as marble figures. We selected a good quantity of all kinds for Susan's basket, then began making our way back through the market as the crowd thickened around us.

The air changed, and suddenly I felt slightly out of breath. Nothing severe – but the feeling was one that signalled the arrival of something greater, like the gentle roll of thunder one believes one hears when the sky is turning grey. I think on it now, and I say I was aware of it, though there is nothing I could have done to better prepare myself for what was coming.

The people were moving in great streams through the market. The persimmon would be in one of the fruit stalls further down. Susan nudged ahead and in seconds I had lost track of her, her hat becoming submerged in the sea of bobbing heads and shifting countenances.

Then I heard it. I did not need to turn around to know what it was.

'Miss Braithwhite.'

He might have touched my shoulder, but I could not be entirely sure. All that matters is that when I turned to face him, he stood there gleaming, like some deity amidst a swarm of his worshippers.

'Mr Rivers,' I said, doing my best to maintain my calm.

He wore a silk hat, a tightly cut velour coat, and the shiniest and most elegantly fitting pair of black gloves. He looked at me. And with that knowing, knowing look, I immediately felt – guilty. I had to be imagining it. He could not possibly have been aware of everything I had just been discussing with Mr Ismay.

'What an unexpected pleasure,' he said.

'Indeed, Mr Rivers. Though your correspondences have intimated that you'd be returning to us soon. And we – that is my brother and I, as well as mother – have been so much looking forward to that.'

'Have you?' he said.

'Well . . . yes,' I stumbled.

'Well, here I am,' he said, grinning. 'And here, as anywhere, my only wish is to do your bidding. May I walk with you? Are you alone, Miss Braithwhite?'

I looked at him. Something told me that he already knew the answer.

'Susan is up ahead,' I said. 'But I will find her. We were already set upon where we were going.'

'And where is that?'

'To collect some persimmon,' I said. 'Mrs Dawes plans to make a pie.'

We began to walk, and Mr Rivers stood beside me. He was tall, and something happened when he took his position. Perhaps it was my imagination, but as we walked, the shape of the crowd seemed to shift, as if his presence, in escorting me, were directing people to move out of my way.

'And how was your journey?' I asked.

'Pleasant,' he said. 'I left very early this morning, and have only just arrived.'

'Ah, John will be so glad to see you,' I said. 'But I assume you are on your way to the office, as matters there must be your top concern.'

I felt him shift, though there was no change in his pace.

'The office is of course my top concern, Miss Braithwhite,' he said. 'But so are you.'

I was somewhat startled.

'Me, Mr Rivers?' I said. 'I can't think what you mean.'

'I mean you – and your family. You are every bit as much of a concern to me as anything that might be going on in the office.'

The crowd thinned and thickened, undulating unevenly as we walked. Susan was up ahead somewhere, though I could still not see where she was.

'Have you been to the office, then?' he asked. 'This morning?'

He knew that I had been. I don't know how he knew, but he did.

'Yes,' I said.

'To look for me?'

'Well, no Mr Rivers, I—'

'The office is buttoned up, I assure you. You can pay a visit any day that you like, at any time of year, and whether I am there or not, the gears will be turning exactly as they should be.'

I did not respond, but he must have seen me stiffen.

'I assure you,' he said. 'It's true.'

'I do not doubt it,' was my reply.

'Does your brother?'

My brother. I could not tell him where I had gone, or what I had learned. He would have said that I shouldn't have been meddling.

'Oh no – no, Mr Rivers,' I said. 'Have I somehow given you that impression?'

'No.'

I sensed that he had turned to look at me, but I did not adjust my gaze.

'My brother has every faith in you,' I said, 'and is deeply grateful for your counsel.'

We continued our walk, and I at last spied Susan some distance ahead. She had stopped to wait along the arcade, in front of one of the confectionery shops. Soon we approached, and Mr Rivers acknowledged Susan, and turned his eyes towards the colourful offerings in the window. The shop's display was filled with every kind of indulgence – blue and white petits fours, sugar-coated nuts, marzipans, chocolate bonbons, and bowls of bright red candied cherries.

'Delicious,' Mr Rivers observed, somewhat randomly. 'Shall we?'

Susan and I followed him into the store – he had not waited for our permission – and inside it was bright, with everything around us sparkling like snow frost. There were heaps of sugared delicacies everywhere on beautiful porcelain trays. The air was sweet. I was hungry.

We browsed, Susan and I off to one side, Mr Rivers off to another. He appeared intent on finding something, and at the same time detached from his purpose. I wondered if I had offended him by going to the office. But more significantly, I wondered how he had discovered so quickly that I had gone there. Truthfully, my objective had not been to check up on him, and certainly I'd had no intention of 'looking for him'.

He was nearing one of the front counters, and I edged myself away from Susan. As I drew near him, I could not help but observe the fine line of his posture.

'Mr Rivers,' I said, 'I did mean what I said a few moments ago – about my brother. That he has every faith in you, as do I.'

He did not look at me, but rather kept his eyes fixed on yet more piles of candied fruit – greens and oranges and reds, brightly illuminated, and shimmering in wet syrup.

'I thank you for saying so, Miss Braithwhite,' he said. 'That is very important to me, given the place I am expected to fill.'

There was a downturn in his voice, and I thought he might be growing melancholy.

'Well, Mr Luckhurst took care of things,' I offered. 'Of everything – for everyone. It is difficult to measure the extent of his influence.'

Mr Rivers was staring vacantly now.

'It certainly is,' he said.

A bell rang, and a woman with two noisy children made her way through the door. My head turned in their direction.

'But the old sod got what he deserved.'

A light flashed, and my startled head whipped back towards Mr Rivers. He was fixated on the fruit bowls, his face still, his eyes staring. For a moment I could not breathe. He could not have said what I had just heard. He could not have possibly said such an odious thing.

But did he?

Susan approached. I looked at Mr Rivers. He turned to me and smiled, his lips aglow, his eyes a-sparkle.

'Aren't they?' he said.

I opened my mouth to speak, but nothing came.

'Aren't they?' he repeated.

'What, Mr Rivers?'

'The apricots,' he said. 'Aren't they beautifully preserved?'

I stared into his eyes, and for a moment saw something terrible – an infinitely patient and crafty creature, smiling, but with a vicious heart. My own heart was shocked, and beat heavily inside me. But at the very second he had darkened, so too had his whole being grown brilliant once again. I was mad. Surely I was out of my mind to have thought him capable of such indiscretion. How could I have!

I tried to regain myself while Mr Rivers beckoned one of the shopkeepers. As I stood there, silent, he ordered an assortment of the most expensive candied sweets for mother and John.

'Such beautiful things, miss,' Susan observed.

But it was difficult for me to comprehend her. The light feeling in my head did not want to go away, and the colours of the confections were making me dizzy.

We all exited the shop, and Mr Rivers handed me the package. I passed the thing on to Susan. I was too ashamed to look at him.

'I will come to see your brother soon,' Mr Rivers said. 'We have much to discuss. And the reports from Devon are – extraordinary.'

'He will be glad to hear it,' I said, somewhat awkwardly. Even those simple words did not come easily.

'Off to fetch the persimmon then?' Mr Rivers asked.

He was staring at me.

'Why yes, Mr Rivers, that we are,' Susan replied.

Then Susan and I turned, expecting him to follow, but Mr Rivers gently stepped in the other direction and tipped his hat towards the both of us.

'Good day, Susan,' he said in the most cordial tone.

Then he looked at me again.

'And you, Miss Braithwhite – do take care.'

The words shocked me, for again he was saying something that felt uncanny. He backed away from us, turned, and within moments was lost in the crowd. Who was this man, this Julian Rivers, and what in heaven's name was he about?

I needed to get home. I was growing more anxious. My mind was racing with terrible questions, and I was desperate to be alone to think.

VIII

A FEW DAYS passed, and I regained my sensibility, and of course mentioned nothing to anyone about the horrible words I thought I had heard escape from Mr Rivers. No, no . . . I could not have heard them. To admit such a thing would have been preposterous. Only I – I – could have been the one who was confused.

John was well, but Henry was not. Poor Henry had begun pulling out some of his feathers. Well, 'some' is not entirely descriptive enough, as he had started with some, but the plucking soon grew to include more and more. It seemed to have happened all of a sudden, overnight – two unseemly patches of naked skin beneath his wings, ugly and rubbery, like the sagging flesh of something dead. The odd behaviour concerned us greatly. He had started drinking in excess too. Every time we looked, his water dish was empty, no matter how many times Susan or I refilled it.

I remember this so clearly because – and I hope you'll forgive me, as I know I've stressed it before, but it's important in terms of what was about to come – I remember poor Henry's decline so clearly because it coincided so perfectly with my brother's revival. With the exception of that one terrible night that followed those first few visits from Mr Rivers, John had rebounded to a shocking degree. And it was noteworthy because the rebound was so unprecedented.

Having tended to John's illnesses since he was a young man, we naturally assumed that his general condition would only worsen over time, and that we'd eventually need to accept whatever grim fate was in store for him. But the opposite now seemed true: John's look, manner, mood – everything about him – had grown as strong and inspiring as it had been when we were children. Even mother, who was the most pessimistic of the lot of us, and who, over the years, had often dismissed John's brief recovery periods as 'untrustworthy', started to entertain the notion that John might be turning some kind of corner. There was something different about him this time, she said – something extraordinary. 'I never thought I'd see the day,' she whispered to me one night, 'when your brother might take his full place at the company, but in these past weeks he has grown into a different person entirely. It's as if someone has given him a potion, and the potion has erased it all.'

Would that it had been so. Well, to have had such a potion at least. It pains me to say it, especially now, but at the time all signs pointed to the potion being somehow connected to Mr Rivers. Poor Henry. All of this is so tangled. But I am telling the truth in proclaiming that, just as Henry's decline seemed to coincide with John's revival, John's revival coincided with this period of increased contact with our new manager. For that's what the rest of that October became – a series of visits and conversations and dinners and revitalisations, all in the presence of the glorious Rivers. Mr Rivers would usually arrive in the late mornings, after breakfast, and stay an hour or so, to discuss business. But there were other days when he might also call later in the afternoon. And then, of course, there were the evening visits too. What was remarkable about the whole thing was the degree to which my brother was able to engage in all matters of the company. Mr Rivers proffered everything, and John absorbed every detail. In my mind, our manager had become a kind of medicine for John, as well as someone John had grown to adore.

It might seem an excessive word – 'adore' – but it is the right one. For that's what I was observing in terms of the relationship developing between them. And who wouldn't adore Mr Julian Rivers? There was, on the surface of things, everything to admire in him – the intelligence and the circumspection; the dedication and sense of duty; the deep understanding of whatever was most difficult; the tempered smiles that brought an inexplicable sense of comfort. We were all quite spellbound by him at the time, even mother, and I will admit – and only here, because again it brings me great shame – but I will admit that whenever John dismissed me from the room so that he and Mr Rivers could conduct their business, an intense jealousy would creep up into my cheeks and flush me red.

One night there was a dinner – about three weeks after Mr Rivers's return from Devon – and it was the night that we were to introduce him to the Stapleton-Graces. He arrived only moments after they did (the Stapleton-Graces always arrived early), and stood at the door of the drawing room like a lord before his vassals. Amongst us he was the lowest in station, and yet his bearing was such that he could have ruled over us all. The power, I realised, came from what he knew – and as I believe I have said before, the way he seemed to understand things. The Stapleton-Graces had been asking for an introduction for weeks. *They* understood that a new manager could possibly lead to all sorts of transformations, both good and bad, and it was an annoyance to them that it had taken so long to meet him.

Mrs Stapleton-Grace was charmed on the spot, while Mr Stapleton-Grace initially played the part of the wary and evaluative elder.

'Rivers,' he said. 'Astonishing, as I've heard, what you've done with the company, in so little time, and with so little experience at the wheel.'

Mr Rivers of course graciously offered that he had done nothing astonishing whatsoever, but had simply executed upon what he had been trained to do by his predecessor.

'Well, it's important to know just when to trim the sails, and when not to,' Mr Stapleton-Grace continued. 'Not always a pretty business – mining and papers – though it's got to be pretty in the end.'

'I can assure you,' Mr Rivers said, 'that the watch has passed to the right person.'

'Eyes in the back of your head then, Rivers?'

'Indeed, sir,' Mr Rivers replied.

They went on, and Mr Stapleton-Grace received our manager's responses with visible complacency. I think Mr Stapleton-Grace's greatest objective that evening was to confirm for himself that this 'Rivers' would not take any radical turns, run the company into the ground, or do anything else disastrous of that sort. Mr Rivers defended himself and his positions shrewdly, Mr Stapleton-Grace being no match for someone who had navigated such waters as Mr Rivers had so far. The conversation remained unremarkable right up until the dinner hour, with Mr Stapleton-Grace continuing his interview, and John and Mr Rivers exchanging glances between one another that revealed what they both thought of the exchange.

Then, as expected, Mr Jayne appeared. But instead of announcing dinner, he entered the drawing room, walked over to Mr Rivers, and quietly said:

'Your boy is here, sir. He says it is a matter of urgency.'

Mr Rivers's eyes twinkled, filled with a strange spark of delight. He excused himself while mother and Mrs Stapleton-Grace chatted on, and after a short time returned with a collection of papers in one of his hands.

'Everything all right, Rivers?' Mr Stapleton-Grace said.

Mr Rivers did not answer him, but rather looked at John.

'I am sorry, sir,' Mr Rivers said, holding the papers as if unsure.

'It's all right, Rivers,' John said. 'You may speak plainly.'

Mr Rivers resumed his seat.

'It is a notice, to be run two days from now in *The Times*,' Mr Rivers said. 'A very brief one, but we are named.'

He handed one of the papers to John.

'Named?' Mr Stapleton-Grace said. 'What on earth are you talking about?'

Mother and Mrs Stapleton-Grace stopped chatting, and all our eyes were upon John as he read.

'It's another arsenic notice,' John said. 'And it's as he says – this time we are named.'

'The devil!' exclaimed Mr Stapleton-Grace. 'It's *The Times* you say? Selby is a—'

'Charles,' Mrs Stapleton-Grace interrupted.

The notice could not have been long, as John had perused the whole thing within a minute. He passed the paper to

Mr Stapleton-Grace, who read it over quickly before finally returning it to Mr Rivers.

'Selby has sunk, I tell you,' Mr Stapleton-Grace exclaimed. 'He has been sinking for some time, and he has sunk deeper, yet again. Naming this family in connection with something so odious. It's undignified, ungrateful – despicable.'

Mother and Mrs Stapleton-Grace remained silent. John had his hand to his chin, thinking.

'Mr Rivers,' I said. 'May I?'

Mr Rivers handed me the piece of paper. It contained a short paragraph, out of context – something that would be placed in one of the long columns of *The Times*.

I read.

WALLS OF DEATH

WE ARE AT *this point well aware that it is no uncommon thing for men and women to die, poisoned by the arsenic in their wall-papers. Now, to the roster of growing deaths and illnesses, we add the Clayridge children, all four of whom have perished within the span of two weeks from exposure to the dampened wall-papers in their nurseries. These children suffered the most severe symptoms, and succumbed to the most unimaginable deaths, all while being soothed by the exquisite patterns from that name known round the globe, Braithwhite & Company. The Devon Great Consols, which copper mines the company also happens to own, contain enough arsenic to poison the entire world. And yet the mining continues and companies like these go on fashioning their lethal colours with impunity. How long will these money-hunters be allowed, in pursuit of their game, to vitiate the necessaries of life with the deadliest poisons? When will the medical establishment at last form a committee to look into this insidious problem? Some readers will remember the 'mysterious circumstances' under which Mr John Braithwhite was found at the bottom of one of his own lime kilns, some eighteen years ago, and how that family since then has met with a series of tragic events. Such an industry is fated to reap its own rewards. We can only hope that parliament and the medical community will one day soon open their eyes.*

So there was to be more of it. Now they would be coming for us. And this would be the first time that they would be coming for us directly. I had done my best to protect my brother and our family our whole lives. But the stuff was seeping out – seeping in a direction I could not see. I didn't understand how people could be so unfeeling, and so cruel.

'Despicable, again I say,' Mr Stapleton-Grace huffed. 'These sensationalists – they'll print anything for attention. A bunch of nonsense. A wonder that anyone could possibly believe it.'

'What does it say, Lucy?' mother asked.

'It's libel,' Mr Stapleton-Grace interjected, looking at John and Mr Rivers. 'We may even have enough to sue for damages. I'd love to see Selby have to eat his own words.'

'Lucy,' mother repeated, 'what does it say?'

I looked at mother. She would not understand – or would she?

'You do not want to hear it, mother,' I said.

Mr Rivers took the paper from me and returned it to the bundle.

'Mrs Braithwhite,' he said, 'it is a salacious piece of writing with which I would not deign to spoil your ears.'

'It goes on Saturday?' John said.

'Of course it's going on Saturday,' Mr Stapleton-Grace added. 'Selby wants to maximise the publicity.'

Mr Rivers looked very serious.

'It will not be going at all,' he said.

We all turned towards him, but no one said a word.

'It will not be going,' he repeated. 'You can be sure of it.'

'But – how, Rivers?' John said.

'You must leave that to me,' Mr Rivers replied, 'but there is no time to waste. I must go. The type will be set up by morning.'

Mr Stapleton-Grace continued to bluster about Mr Selby, John remained thoughtful, and mother adopted her familiar face of worry. But Mr Rivers disappeared before Mr Jayne could even announce dinner. What baleful witchery he'd so immediately gone off to work for us – I could not fathom.

That evening, after the Stapleton-Graces had finally departed, and mother had gone up to bed, I returned to the drawing room to sit with John, as was our usual custom. His mind was occupied – naturally so – with the threat of the appearance of such a wretched thing in the papers. He was worried, as was I, of the consequences of the appearance, and what even the hint of a scandal would mean for the company.

But there was more. There was the reality that John and I and mother were all nestled safely in our home, and that out there in the wider world there were dangers beyond our control. My own sleep was quiet. I did not have nightmares. But that was because, at the time, the things that haunted me did not seem so troublesome.

John was contemplative. He was beautiful and strong.

'You see, Lucy,' he said. 'You see how we need him.'

I nodded.

'He has become absolutely necessary to us,' John said.

'I miss Mr Luckhurst,' I said.

'The thing is, Lucy,' John said, rising, 'such immense possibilities have opened. Mr Luckhurst, God rest his soul, could never have revealed the opportunities that now lie before us.'

'Well,' I offered, 'he did sustain us all those years.'

'Yes,' John said, now walking about, 'but that's just it. He sustained us. I feel that with Rivers, we are on the brink of something even more extraordinary. Something father, or Mr Luckhurst, or myself could never have imagined.'

I supposed John might have been referring to the formulas again, but whatever the case, it was the charm of the new.

'He's changing everything,' John said. 'If only you could understand the way he *thinks*. He is getting me to see things differently – to think of them differently. Revealing things. Even in our simplest patterns I'm noticing the splendour of something I have always looked for, but have somehow always missed.'

I felt that I had started to grow pale. A curious sense of terror came over me. My brother – and I – had come face to

95

face with someone whose mere personality was so captivating that it could absorb John's entire nature, if he allowed it to do so.

'I know, John,' I said. 'I do see it – the way he's changed you. It's remarkable, considering how we've only known him a short time.'

'Time has nothing to do with it,' John said. 'The whole thing with Rivers has been a joy. And rightly so. Lord knows this family has had its share of sorrow.'

Henry gurgled – he had been drinking all night – and John walked over and stuck his fingers through the cage to pet him. I had done my best. I had lived to carry John. But now, over him, there had developed another influence – one that I was admittedly jealous of whenever I had to acknowledge how powerful it was. Not that I wanted to do anything to work against it, of course. I only wanted what was best for John – what would make my brother happy.

'Do you think Mr Rivers is fond of us?' I said.

John removed his hand from the cage.

'Lucy,' he said. 'Of course he is fond of us. What a strange question.'

But as he came back towards me, and the fire coloured his face, his expression revealed that he too held some uncertainty. With his attention and admiration, he had flattered Mr Rivers dreadfully, and that alone should have warranted some kind of fondness. But the truth was that neither of us knew what Mr Rivers privately thought. We did not know what he did with his time, or even where he lived. And yet he had come into our house and inserted himself into our family, not because we had 'inherited' him, but because we had invited him in.

John sat back down. There was a subtle look of fear in his eyes.

'I will tell you, Lucy,' he said quietly, 'that at times I find a strange pleasure in telling him things that I know I shall be sorry for having said.'

A horrible sinking feeling crept into my stomach.

'What do you mean?' I asked.

'Just that . . .'

He paused. His lips revealed a slight tremble.

'Well . . .' John stumbled. 'That you are right to ask the question, and that I am not right to be so cavalier with you. We do not know. Our gratitude for what he's brought to us may mean no more to him than the cravat one ties in the morning, or the brand of blacking one uses for one's boots.'

'I don't think it's as low as that,' I said.

'No,' John said. 'There is something.'

I was glad to have John all to myself. That, I was sure, was a circumstance that would never change. Or would it? John had totally revived under the influence of this tall and graceful young man – a man of the world whose expression was as serious and worn as it was fascinating and beautiful. Which, though I hate to admit it, made me afraid of him because he was a stranger, a stranger with great power, and I was afraid of what such a stranger might reveal. I had known and loved my brother for my entire life, and yet in a matter of weeks I had witnessed how easily someone else had altered him. It was as if all this time there had been a mystery lurking behind us, and Mr Rivers had simply come along to disclose it. And yet, what was there to be afraid of? This was what we had always longed for – for John to partake of the 'joys', as he put it, that the rest of us took for granted. How I loved him. And how I loved what Mr Rivers seemed to be doing for him. John was no longer a schoolboy and I was no longer a girl. The company called us. There were great opportunities. It was absurd to be frightened.

But I was.

IX

THAT SATURDAY, WE all awoke with great anticipation of seeing *The Times*, and whether or not Braithwhite & Company would in fact be mentioned in connection with so much scandal. At breakfast, mother and I held our breaths as John slowly paged through the paper, scanning column after column as he went in search of the attack. Mother quietly stirred her tea. She had had a surprisingly good night. And even Henry remained unusually silent that morning, his head nodding as he dozed.

John went through the whole paper, and then returned to the first page.

'Well?' mother said.

John put his hand up to check her. He began leafing through the paper again, this time scanning the columns with one of his fingers. He flipped page after page, and at last reached the end.

'Well?' mother repeated.

'It's not here,' John said.

'Not there?' I said.

'No,' John replied. 'It's not here.'

'Well,' mother said. 'That's an end to that then.'

Just then, Mr Jayne came in and announced Mr Stapleton-Grace. Mr Jayne had himself barely entered the room when the other man barged in behind him.

'I'm sorry to interrupt your breakfast,' he said, waving his own copy of *The Times* before us, 'but you've seen it, I gather?'

'I've just gone through it,' John said.

'Extraordinary!' Mr Stapleton-Grace exclaimed. 'Not a word of it to be found.'

'No, not a word,' John said. 'I don't know how he did it.'

'It's extraordinary,' Mr Stapleton-Grace repeated. 'Seems like you wound up with a good captain of the ship after all. Any man who can go head-to-head with Selby is a man I want to know.'

'Yes,' mother said flatly, 'Mr Rivers is extraordinary.'

'But how on earth did he do it?' John asked. 'The type was practically set up. And Selby does not back down.'

'Does it matter?' mother said.

'Selby's a scandal monger,' Mr Stapleton-Grace said, 'but he's no fool. He knows that it would not have been prudent for him to have run that notice as it was written.'

'Prudence never seems to have concerned him in the past,' my brother said. 'What he did last year with the Carmichaels – it was ghastly. Thank heavens for Lucy it all turned out the way it did.'

Mother and Mr Stapleton-Grace both glanced at me. It was not common for any of us to mention Mr Carmichael.

'Perhaps Mr Rivers understands Selby better than we know,' Mr Stapleton-Grace said.

And he tapped a finger to the table.

'When it comes to certain things.'

John nodded, and mother breathed. No more needed to be said. There were rumours about Mr Selby, not discussed widely of course, but talked about in certain circles nonetheless. He was, for a man in his position, said to have – well, certain faults of character. And one could believe it, as he was one of those men in London who was friend to everyone, and enemy to all. He had even, I think, been to the house for dinner once or twice when I was girl – a guest of Mr Luckhurst's who must have been courting him about something or other. But rumours, as we know, are damaging, whether there is truth to them or not, and even though Mr Selby was often entertained at the greatest houses, the best families always made sure to keep their proper distance.

I was never the one in our family to have visions, at least not then, but for some strange and awful reason, a peculiar vision struck me in that moment. I did not need to hear even a suggestion of how Mr Rivers might have helped us, for the scene unfolded entirely before me, as clear as the moving pictures from a magic lantern. There is Mr Selby, his portly figure visible in the rippled windows of an alehouse. And here comes Mr Rivers – tall, handsome, his clothes pristine, his mind intent on his singular mission. He enters the alehouse and approaches the ill-tempered Selby, and the two men begin their conversation. At first, their talk is cordial; they could be chattering about the weather, the city, the Thames. From the street one sees them nod and smile – all gentlemanly pleasantry to start. But then Mr Rivers asks something of Mr Selby, and the face of Mr Selby changes. He grows defiant. He pounds the table. He orders Mr Rivers to be gone! Mr Rivers asks again – would the gentleman reconsider? And again Mr Selby, in a huff, tells his companion that the thing is already done.

Mr Rivers, patient, asks a third time if Mr Selby would be so kind as to reverse his course of action. The good name of an important family and the reputation of an entire company are at stake, and Mr Selby, he says, will be compromising that name and that company.

But Mr Selby, with his most dramatic gesture yet, dismisses Mr Rivers, and returns to his reading.

Mr Rivers does not react. He is as still as a fox in the woods. Mr Selby does not bother to look up as Mr Rivers takes a pen and paper from his own coat pocket.

Ah – how elegant the hand of Mr Rivers must be! He writes something. He reads it. He lets the ink dry. Then he folds the piece of paper and pushes it across the table.

Mr Selby looks up. He is hesitant. He does not immediately take the paper. A slow and sinking feeling creeps into him, for he is surmising what the piece of paper says. He takes the paper, opens it, reads it. And to his horror it contains the worst words he can imagine.

There is a pause. Then, Mr Rivers speaks a few words. But even before that, one can see that Mr Selby has been defeated. Again, from the street, looking through the alehouse window, this startling picture is so clear before me. Mr Selby sinks his head into the palms of his two fat hands, and Mr Rivers stands up, wishes him good day, and leaves.

Yes, I know the whole display is fanciful and unpleasant. But in my mind there is no other explanation for what happened. For nothing could have derailed a man as staunch as Mr Selby, unless such a man were faced with something that compromised him totally. We all have our secrets. We understand their importance. And we know the lengths we must – and do – go to keep them.

X

THE NEXT DAY, we received Mr Rivers for dinner. It was foggy that evening, with a dull drizzle of October rain, and layers of misty wisps rolling in and surrounding the house. There was that feeling, and if I looked out and squinted just enough, I could make the lines of the city vanish, and replace them with curves and streams.

It was a melancholy evening, both outside and in, but the arrival of Mr Rivers brought about a change in mood. We all knew what had happened, and were all quite relieved, and though there was no direct mention of what had taken place, there were many thank yous on both John and mother's part. I had asked Mrs Dawes to prepare a pheasant that evening, along with a few other special things to mark the occasion. And Susan had come back the day before with a lovely box of candied cherries, their bright red skins glistening and sparkling like wet rubies. We would serve them alongside almond cake with Chantilly cream – something that Mr Rivers had once remarked he liked very much.

The particulars of what we ate that night are rather important, as you shall see, for they instigated the opening of a door that I would have preferred to have left closed.

The evening itself turned out to be generally pleasant, Mr Rivers being only good news and optimism throughout. The meal advanced leisurely, the candles lowered and glowed, and by the time the dinner plates had been cleared away, the sordid thing that had been worrying us had, for the moment, retreated sufficiently into the background.

'And we are going,' John said, 'we are going up-up-up. Didn't think there was anywhere else to go, but with Rivers, the skies have widened.'

'It seems as though you've situated the company very well,' mother added. 'And as I move into my last years, it gives me great solace to see that my late husband's work, and his father's before him, has come to pass into such capable hands.'

'Mother, there's no need to be morbid,' John said.

'Well, it's true,' mother said. 'There is always uncertainty about the morrow. And to know that there are – well, guardians at the gates. This is what a mother hopes for.'

She was flattering him on purpose – performing for him again. And I was reasonably sure that he understood those kinds of things. But with all of that flattering and performing and understanding, it's still shameful to me that I myself had yet to grasp mother's true intentions.

'It pleases me greatly to hear that you think of me as such,' Mr Rivers said.

He took a large swig of Madeira, and smiled at John.

'I do,' mother said. 'This company has always had its guardians. Its . . . well, its future, for so many, is too important to be left unguarded.'

Out came the almond cake, the Chantilly cream, the candied cherries. It was all going so well. But then, I couldn't help myself.

'Is there,' I said, 'anything you are intending to do about the formulas?'

John and Mr Rivers glanced at one another.

'I'm sorry?' Mr Rivers said.

I looked at him. He was smiling at me.

'I am simply asking the question,' I said. 'Are you intending to do anything about the formulas?'

John cleared his throat.

'Why do you ask, Lucy?'

'I have just heard mention,' I said, 'on many occasions, this or that about the formulas, and I was wondering what all of that might mean. For the company.'

'The formulas don't really concern us, Lucy,' mother said, quietly.

'But they do, mother,' I said. 'The formulas concern this whole family. There are, I am guessing, many out there who would like nothing more than to see us bend to changing our formulas. With all that's being said lately, in the papers.'

Mr Rivers was still smiling.

'I hope you know, Miss Braithwhite,' he said, 'that I would never do anything that would compromise the company – or this family.'

'The formulas—' I began.

But John stopped me.

'You see what's going on out there, Lucy,' he said. 'You see what they are trying to do to us. We must . . . well, we must *enhance* our formulas, by any means necessary, if we are to stay on top. We have never, and will never, surrender to public sentiment, especially absurd public sentiment of the kind that is going around.'

Mr Rivers nodded, as if he could not have come up with better words himself.

'So you *are* considering changing the formulas then,' I said. 'But not to accommodate the situation.'

Then the man stopped smiling. And for the second time now, I noticed something like a touch of cruelty creep into the lines of his mouth. He pressed the tip of his spoon into one of his cherries. The skin broke, the china clanked, and the fruit slid clear across his plate.

'The matter is – slippery,' he said, his voice golden. 'One needs to take care where one treads.'

He was looking straight at me. Blood rushed through my limbs. The walls around me started to gyrate, and I could only stop them from spinning by staring down at my own spoon. What was he doing? Had the wine gone to my head? Across from me, Mr Rivers was at once larger and further away than I expected.

He knew.

But how could he? It had happened over ten years ago, and he had had nothing whatsoever to do with our lives back then. I had been hurrying up the back staircase myself with a plate of sweets for Tom, and had stumbled, and a few of the very same candied cherries had rolled about. I had not picked all of them up, and yet it had not been my fault when Tom's nurse, Mary Toole, later slipped and fell and died. At the time it was all very serious, with Susan proclaiming that it had finally happened – that the back stairs, uneven as they were, had been the end of 'one of them that's forced to use 'em'. But I remember thinking, as unfeeling as it might seem to say, that Mary Toole was an awful thing, with her superstitions and her theories. She was, after all, the one wanting

106

to take Tom out of the house. It was unhealthy, she said. The whole reason for his constant decline. As if the house were what was really trying to kill him.

How had he seen it? How had he known what had happened? Did Mr Rivers have a magic lantern of his own?

My brother leapt up from his chair.

'Lucy!' he exclaimed. 'Are you all right?'

He was holding me – I had started to fall – and my dessert spoon had dropped to the ground. My head pounded, and a hollow sound rang in my ears. But just as quickly as the whole thing had come on, it was gone.

I pressed my eyes.

'Yes,' I said. 'Yes, thank you. I am fine.'

Then John released me, but stayed close.

'Perhaps Miss Braithwhite needs to go upstairs,' Mr Rivers said.

'Miss Braithwhite needs nothing of the kind,' I said, recovering.

I was angry. And in that moment, I had – yes – the sudden urge to strike him.

In the glow of the candlelight, the room had come to a halt, and Mr Rivers had once again grown virtuous. There was nothing I could do. For what could I say against him? This creature who had descended into our lives, and whom my mother and my brother seemed to adore more and more each day. Yes, I knew mother was only half sincere in her praises of him, but in my mind the three of them had started to form a kind of collective – a collective into which I might not neatly fit.

And then I had a horrible thought: perhaps he wanted *me* out of the house.

Mother yawned. The wines had been a little too much for all of us. We left the table, ascended the stairs, and went into the drawing room together. Before long, mother declared her need to retire, so I accompanied her to her room while John and Mr Rivers remained alone together. Mother was – complacent. Yes, a strange word to use for her, but that, I think, is what she was. It was not just the wine. There was something else to it, accompanied by a girlish smile on her face. As I helped her into her bedclothes, she was completely without distress. For once, I could sense no signs of her usual torments.

Indeed, the man could cast spells.

But something else had happened. He had poked at me now, and wanted me to understand that he knew things. Knew things about me, about the company, about our family, that no one else was supposed to have known. And the worst of it was that he was unpredictable and indirect about all of this, like a snake moving slyly from one spot to another, ready to stay his course – or bite.

Once mother was safely asleep, I went back down to the drawing room, only to find Mr Rivers in the hall, exiting John's room alone.

'Mr Rivers?' I questioned.

He put a finger to his lips. He was quietly closing the door behind him.

'Your brother has retired,' he whispered. 'He could not stay awake. He was stumbling around a bit and I helped him into bed.'

I managed a smile. I did not want to strike him any more. But I'll admit, I was not at all pleased to be looking at him.

'That was very kind of you,' I said.

He returned the look of pleasantry and we silently stole down the stairs together, forced into an agreement of quietness. Susan, thank goodness, was downstairs in the kitchen with Mrs Dawes. At the front door, Mr Rivers collected his hat and his gloves.

'Good evening, Miss Braithwhite,' he said.

Even with what I was feeling, the eyes were impossible not to admire.

'Good evening, Mr Rivers.'

He was gazing at me intently, and I at him. We stood motionless, and I was determined not to back down. His eyes sparkled. They were beautiful – disturbingly beautiful. I could not move my own eyes from his, and yet the sensation within me was one of growing sickness and of horror.

He should have turned to go, but didn't. I wanted him to go. We were locked, and then – one corner of his mouth and the top of his brow raised. Not a twitch or even a smile, but a hideous invitation.

'I understand you now, Mr Rivers,' I finally said.

The brow softened, the mouth relaxed.

'It makes me glad to hear it,' he replied.

'And I think we understand each other.'

'I think we do.'

'Then I must ask you to speak frankly with me,' I said. 'I am going to ask you a question that I have never asked anyone. I am going to ask, for the sake of everyone in this house, that you bring me into your confidence, as I know you have brought my brother.'

'I am only here to serve you,' Mr Rivers said.

'Then as a true . . . servant,' I said, 'I must ask you . . .'

He was still.

'What is it?' I said.

'What is what, Miss Braithwhite?'

'What is it – that we *do*?'

His face fell for a moment, and I could not tell whether he was displeased or relieved. The eyes still shone and the lips still glistened. Then his mouth broke into a gentle smile, and he said, as if in answer:

'Ah – what we do.'

His brow deepened, and I was filled with that same emotion that I experienced on the first day I had met him. Somehow, looking into the eyes of this devil, I was ready to believe anything he would tell me.

'You do not know,' he said.

'I do not,' I replied.

'And you want to know,' he said. 'Because it has become a burden not to know.'

His face was very serious, but the mouth was still full of amusement.

'I need to know what's true,' I said. 'If there is any truth to any of this whatsoever.'

He smiled.

'I can tell you what is true,' he said, 'though what many have said is far from true.'

'Please,' I said.

He paused, intentionally. I had begged him. He had delighted in it.

At last he said:

'The truth is that there exists no green pigment so beautiful and unfading as ours – the one we produce from copper arsenite, which we of course derive from our own mines.'

The breath caught in my chest. I tried not to hold onto it. My next words were automatic – unthinking.

'And this is a problem?' I spat out.

'Some say so,' he replied.

Then he added:

'I do not say so.'

He was scolding me for even asking, as if my stupidity had got the better of me. I was as gullible as all those fools writing and reading the notices in the papers.

'But that is not the whole of it,' he said.

I urged him to go on.

'When mixed with other colours for toning – blues, yellows, reds, even browns – the arsenic imbues everything with a colour that is fresh and clear. There is no denying it. The superiority of it is unquestionable. Compare a blue that contains no arsenic to a blue that contains even the tiniest quantities, and you will see a colour that's been kissed beside a colour that's been forsaken.'

'You are saying, then,' I offered, 'that we enhance more than the greens.'

'Precisely,' he replied. 'The greens were only the beginning. Once we discovered the magical effects of the chemical, the temptation to enhance all of our colours became very strong, because the additive imparted a delicacy and shading to *every* colour. And here is where we had – have – the advantage over all the others, because the substance is too costly for our competitor friends to use indiscriminately.'

It did not sound so dire.

'And John,' I said. 'He is aware of this advantage?'

'Miss Braithwhite,' Mr Rivers said, 'what I've told you is no secret, complicated as it is. But in my view, over time, the whole thing can be made even more advantageous.'

I was not entirely sure what he meant, and I did not want to ask. In that moment, shamefully, I had become like mother in thinking that – or at least pretending to think that – the formulas had nothing to do with us. I wish I had understood then the monstrosity of what he was proposing. I might have pressed him. I might have been able to put an end to all of it sooner.

Then he added:

'And as far as your brother and I go – well, that's the least of it.'

Once again, I had lost. I was establishing a pattern of defeat with him. And it unsettled me that in my ignorance I had no choice but to bow to him. The sly manner with which he dismissed my enquiry about my brother was designed to pierce straight through my skin and into my heart. He had knowledge of us – not just of me and mother and John, but of all of us who were here now, and who had come before.

'But none of this should cause you any worry, Miss Braithwhite,' he added. 'Or your family. I can assure you, you have never been in a safer place.'

A viper curled in a cave might hiss a warning before it strikes, and likewise this concluding expression from Mr Rivers was intended to convey anything but reassurance. There was no doubt in my mind that, somewhere along the way, Mr Rivers had determined to control everything. And in the process of controlling everything, he would *take* everything – the formulas, the company, our dignity, John. Fool that I am, I allowed him to take my hand before he bowed his goodbye and descended our front steps. His horse snorted under his weight, a beast subjugated by this master, and the blurred flames of the street lamps looked ghastly in the dripping mist. Then the master, hungrier and more deliberate than ever before, rode off into the dark night, as if he hunted women and men.

All was silent after he left. The hall clock chimed to mark the late hour. I looked for Henry in the drawing room, but Mr Rivers must have taken him along with John into John's room. Now and then, a sound escaped from down below – Susan and Mr Jayne tidying things up after the last of the evening's activities.

I retired to my room. The cold from the front door had followed me. In a while, I heard Susan quietly ascending to her own room upstairs.

I did not dream, because dreaming was a thing I rarely did, but as I lay there in the dark, a rapid stream of thoughts rushed through me. How had Mr Rivers come to discover all that he knew? A man so young, and from such humble upbringing – a man who had simply materialised from the atmosphere around us? I wondered if he had made some perfidious bargain in order to become the man he was, and hated to let myself even think of what the terms of that bargain might have been. Whatever the case, the air had cleared, and the threat of his presence now stood before me. On Dartmoor, we knew, the sheep could graze without fear of harm. Our great-grandfather had been amongst those men intent on exterminating the last of the wolves. But even after all those beautiful predators had met their violent ends, was the threat of destruction ever really gone?

Could you ever be sure? Could you gambol freely up those boulder-sprinkled hills, or round a nab of heath without any cause for fear?

We were not safe. The winged serpents that frequented the hills may have been the stuff of legend, but the wolves that inhabited the valleys were real, and now one of them had returned.

I was sure of it.

My sleep was restless. My thoughts would not stop. The warmth from the coal fire was the only thing that brought comfort. I fell in and out of slumber like a denned creature in the grey hours before dawn. Then I heard it – a horrible shriek, half human, half something else. A shrill cry that pierced the stagnant night.

I lit the candle, put on my dressing gown, and went out into the hall. All was quiet. Mother breathed softly and regularly through the panels of her fastened door. The hall clock whispered from down below. There was nothing out of place, either upstairs or down.

I listened. I was sure of what I had heard. I stepped out into the hall. The walls glowed in the feeble light.

Then the sound came again – a hideous scream. Inhuman! It had travelled up from the floor below. It had come from John's room. It was happening again.

I raced down the stairs, the flame of the candle licking towards me. What monster had crept into our house? What beast had broken in to devour my brother? I had saved him from everything – from the world, from death itself. If a new foe had advanced upon us, then let it come and let me see it!

I threw open John's door, expecting to find some demon over his bed – one of the ancient moorland dragons, teeth gnashing, eyes on fire. But what confronted me when I fell into the room was a scene so disturbing, that at once an unknown kind of fear overcame me. I gasped. I could do nothing but swallow the horrible sight with my stifled breath.

The room was cold, for one of the windows was wide open, and the dampness in the air heightened the chill. One of the lamps had been lit – the lamp at John's bedside – and so the room was aglow in the cold night air, any warmth from the fire giving up its effects to the encroaching wind. My brother stood facing the wall in front of his bed, all of his clothes removed, his pale skin a bright light before father's green paper. He was motionless. His back was to me. He stood as if frozen. I moved into the room, moved closer to John with the candle, to find him staring, his lips un-parted, his eyes two possessed globes of glass.

Then Henry screeched – the loudest cry he ever made. I had never heard a sound so otherworldly and wretched. He was gurgling – choking – and at this sound John gasped too. My brother coughed once, then coughed again, and soon he was gasping and choking, like the bird.

I tore the covers from the bed and threw them over my brother. He sank to the floor, his breathing heavy as he tried to catch his breath. The cold was dreadful. I closed the open window and John clutched at his throat. The blankets made for clumsy robes, and slipped from his naked shoulders.

'John!' I exclaimed, going down to him, covering him. 'John my love . . .'

I wrapped my arms around him. He was heaving like a dying animal.

'John!' I repeated. 'John – John!'

His face was twisted, as if he wanted to cry but couldn't. He was as cold as the night air around us. I tightened the bedclothes around him, and he held them close about his chin. His breathing slowed. I stayed with him. He trembled as I held him.

We remained like that for quite a long time – though how long I cannot say. Gradually the steady pace of his breathing returned, and his eyelids drooped as he quieted.

'John,' I said, 'you must never, ever open the window. Never again!'

I imagined he would protest – some defence about how he could not breathe. But as soon as I had scolded him, I realised that he was not the one who had opened the window.

I smoothed his hair, brushed the cold strands from his forehead. His head fell onto my breast and I held him. He was a man, who had been schooled and who had grown to learn and understand things. And yet, how small he felt in my arms – a child that would never live to grow.

'You've seen it,' I finally said.

Startled, he raised his head.

'Lucy!' he exclaimed. 'You know – you've always known!'

'The vision comes at night,' I said. 'But the picture is much more than a dream. It was the same way with Tom.'

John let out a silent cry.

'All these years!' he said. 'Lucy – am I mad?'

'You are not mad, my dear brother,' I answered.

He sat up a little on his own, and adjusted the blankets again.

'You've seen it too, then? You've seen them?'

I did not answer. He was seeing what poor Tom had seen. The vision – the children.

We waited.

'It was horrible,' he said.

'I know, John.'

'They could not breathe.'

'I know.'

'Down there in the darkness. Children – barely men. Their faces blackened. Crying – screaming!'

'Insomuch as they could,' I said. 'Before—'

My own candle flickered. The shadows in the wall's patterns stretched and groaned. Something was crying out, and something had got back in. Mr Rivers, in his magnificent efficiency, had made sure of that. He knew what was in the paper and he knew that it would not stay silent. The question was, had *he* awakened it? Or worse yet – was he somehow infernally at one with it? My inclination was to believe no . . . even he was not so powerful. But whatever the case, his entrance into our lives was unquestionably tangled up with everything that John was now seeing.

I got John back into bed and placed his nightclothes beside him. He was already cocooned in the sheets and would fall asleep that way. The window was closed, the fire would warm the damp, and my sweet brother would be left to slumber.

But as John slowly faded, and I made my last fixes, I realised that Henry had been silent since that last scream. I took the candle to the cage. The cage's shadow grew upon the wall. I looked up at it, the fine bars slashing across the pattern.

Then I peered down.

'Henry—'

The bird was dead.

What horror welled inside me at that moment I can barely describe. The forces were rising, coming to take things again, hungry and unfed, clamouring for air. It was a conspiracy, I thought – a horrible plot against our family to seize from us what was most vulnerable and beloved. The quiet we had enjoyed for so many years was once again crumbling, and if I had dreamed at all, it was to the tune of the deception that the quiet would remain. But John – my dearest and most precious brother, I have survived this before, and I know what to expect. I will keep you safe. I will bring light to these shadows. The war is approaching, but this time they will not win.

XI

ON DARTMOOR, THAT group of stones we called the 'six children' had been our favourite playmates. And why shouldn't they have been? We had no one else to play with, as father would not allow us to mingle with any of the children in the village. John and I had discovered the six children alone together before Tom, and then as Tom grew over the years, we took him to see them too. They lived (and I do use that word intentionally) perhaps half an hour's walk from the house, in a little valley that, depending on the season, had the friendliest brook running through it. Friendly as it all seemed, though, the soil in that area was swampy, and covered with bog moss, so one needed to take extra care. The six children, fortunately, were situated on a dry spot – slightly raised from the rest – and there they had stood strong, waiting for us, I liked to think, for many thousands of years.

There are those phrases from one's childhood that become lodged in one's memory like a splinter just under the skin. (Father's 'There are bogs. There are dangers' was, for me, one of them.) And on that same day of the accident – I was nearly six, and John was eight, and Tom had just been born – a phrase came out of mother, the tone and colour of which I can never forget.

It was this:

'Those poor children.'

John and I had been gone all morning, roaming the hills, and had returned to the moor's edge near the house. The day had been bright and clear when we started out, but as we made our way home, rain squalls had begun drifting in. The heavy, slate-coloured clouds hung low over the melancholy horizon, and I remember looking back over the picture as one turns a final time to bid farewell. Ah – that brooding sky, those deadened colours, those grey wreaths of clouds trailing down the sides of the fantastic hills! The freedom was out there and the air was clear. Our child's paradise, despite the danger.

We came in through the back kitchen, John and I, and sensed a strange feeling in the house. One of the cooks was stirring something, but she took no notice of us, and we none of her, and we proceeded to the front parlour where the small crowd was assembled. Mother was in there, sitting, and next to her was Mary Toole, holding Tom, and father was standing over by the mantel with Mr Luckhurst, as well as one or two other men from the company.

Mother whispered the words as we came in.

'Those poor children.'

There was, as I said, the strangest feeling in the air – the same feeling you get when you stare into a thunderous storm, petrified by its ferocity and yet unable to tear your eyes away from it. The men were all dour. Something had changed.

Only fragments of the words that defined the conversation remain for me. Perhaps more remain for John, though I've never asked. In my little mind, though, I remember thinking for a moment that mother, along with us, understood the six children – cold, weather-beaten, and sad in their isolation. Standing strong and held together by nothing else but each other.

'How many?' one of the men said.

'Ten,' answered another. 'Perhaps fifteen. They are still trying to count.'

There were grimaces, feet shuffling. Many moments of complete silence.

'The report was clear.'

'And you still ordered them to go down?'

That last had been Mr Luckhurst. Father looked at him, unfeelingly.

'And what of it?' he said. 'We couldn't send the men in. The passage was too narrow. We've done it countless times before.'

'But John, we knew—'

'These things happen,' father said. 'The question before us at present is, what do we do about it?'

The feeling in the room now was one of lingering sickness. Some faces were stern, while some were morose.

'Those poor children.'

The Devon house – a country house – had no paper. The rooms were free, unencumbered by bold colour and decoration. Even after the accident, that remained its chief charm. What must mother have been thinking, then, as she looked around at those bare walls? At the company men in their consternation? At her own children as they innocently entered into the room?

Of course, the accident was of no great significance to us when we were children. We barely understood what had happened. But as we grew older, I noticed how it followed us wherever we went – how bits and pieces of it would emerge, and how mother would become upset. Indeed, mother's headaches were usually at their worst whenever suggestion of the accident made its way towards her. By the time I was eleven or twelve I had grown to understand that it was simply best for it to remain unmentioned.

And then, after Tom died, we stopped going down to Devon altogether, and it was much easier for that event's voice to stay silent.

But it didn't. Because Tom – my dear brother – continued to hear and see. Though he barely made it past his eighth year, he *knew*. Knew more than any of us. When I looked at the ambiguous shapes on the walls of his room, I saw nothing more than one of the company's entrancing patterns. But Tom saw those things that the rest of us – or at least I – could not see. That the rest of us, for so long, outright refused to see.

The green colour was bold. The pattern unforgiving. All around, inescapable, were the marks of the company.

But now, before my very eyes, the whole thing was happening all over again – this time with John – and the arrival of it faced me with a terrible dilemma. Mr Rivers, sly creature that he was, had become an essential member of our house and our family. Mother had been oddly captivated by him. John looked upon him as our saviour. And all our fates, as well as that of the company, rested in his hands. On the surface of things, he seemed like our antidote, but the truth was – he was poison. The start of John's visions had coincided perfectly with his arrival, and though Mr Rivers was providing something, he was taking as much as he provided.

And then there were the returns. All anyone could talk about were the returns. But I was beginning to wonder if something wrong or untruthful might lie beneath those too.

So what was I to do? I could not worry John or mother, and I could not honestly alert them to the danger I felt. For the moment, the only thing I could do was step up my guard, and protect John as much as I could from what I was now thinking of as a hateful influence. It was a tricky matter, for as John said, we needed Mr Rivers. In such a short time we had grown to depend on him. Indeed, that had been his whole plan from the beginning.

You can imagine, then, my trepidation when, the day after Henry's death and John's terrible episode, Mr Rivers was the first person my brother called for. John had not come down to breakfast the following morning, which was of course as strange as when he had first started coming down again. John had been doing so well, and the mornings were good for him, and mother and I had, without thinking, come to rely on his company.

But that morning, instead of John, in came Mr Jayne, bearing warmed plates of soft eggs and blood pudding.

No one said anything. Mr Jayne set down the plates.

'Has my brother stirred this morning?' I asked at last.

'Yes, miss,' Mr Jayne answered.

'And – is he coming down?'

'I don't know, miss. The door was locked, and I did not wish to disturb him.'

'But you heard him stirring?'

'Not exactly,' Mr Jayne said.

'Please, Mr Jayne,' I said. 'Speak plainly.'

'Well, miss, as I said, the door was locked and I did not wish to disturb him. But as I turned to go, he called out to me, and asked that I send for Mr Rivers.'

'Mr Rivers!' I gasped. 'You mean my brother called out to you, from his bed?'

'I assume so, miss.'

'For Mr Rivers?'

'Yes, miss.'

'And did you send for him?'

'Well, yes miss. Your brother slipped a note out from under the door, and I sent it.'

The devil would be coming then.

'And has there been a reply?'

'No, miss,' Mr Jayne said. 'I assume he'll just come, as he usually does.'

Mother looked concerned.

'Shall we set a place for him?' she said.

'No, mother,' I snapped. 'We will make a place for Mr Rivers when and if he arrives.'

Mr Jayne left the room, and I was alone with mother. I might as well say that I was alone altogether, though, since no one else around me seemed to understand what was happening. Mr Rivers was to come into the house, and each time he did so, things would worsen. His presence would go on infecting us as he persisted with his plotting. He had bored into us like a weevil, and would continue to sow destruction. That was his pattern. That was his plan.

He did not want me. He wanted John.

He wanted the company.

I had many questions and my mind wandered uncontrollably. The accident – something I had always tried not to think of – was now back, in the form of someone who not only knew about it, but who had referred to it. Well, at least indirectly. My mind could not help but wander – back to the child that I was, back to the six children, back to the lost child I had discovered.

That had been a day or two after the accident. John was a little way off, and I was wandering by myself through a patch of dried heather. I saw the rough boot first, which I initially mistook for a stone, but as I followed the line up, the stone became a leg, then a mass of torn and filthy clothes, and finally a face horribly blackened with grime.

I gasped at the sight of him, jumped back.

It was a dead child, I thought – one of the children father's men had all been talking about. I imagined that the mine had somehow spat this one out, and that this boy had landed here, so that someone might eventually find him.

Oh the horror of it – the sadness!

There were cuts on the boy's hands. The blood was black and dry. His hands were covered in a horrible black, with even darker lines creasing his knuckles.

The child was dead, and someone would need to know about it, because they had been talking in the house so much about 'recovering the lost'. Because you see, most of the children that had been lost in the mine were never recovered. And that was the true horror – for the mothers and the fathers. The passage that collapsed had been unusually narrow, which is why they had sent in the children instead of the men in the first place.

It would take days, they said – weeks, perhaps – for anyone to get through to where the children might still be.

I turned back to look at John. He needed to see this dead child, this thing that the mine had spat out upon the moor.

This dead boy, this strange thing, lying softly in a patch of heather.

Then, as I was about to call for my brother, he shouted my name.

'Lucy!'

He was holding up some sort of rock, to show me.

And then, dreadfully, I heard the ground move beside me. I looked. The boy's eyes had suddenly opened – terrified, and white – amidst the thick black grime that covered his face. Oh – the eyes of that child, so brilliant and white, like lights coming up through two great cracks in the hideous ground!

We looked at each other, my eyes locked upon his. I was terrified. My whole self froze and I could not breathe. Something moved, something shifted – I felt the air shift. I looked around. Not far off, the six children were trembling. And John was as distant from me as a crag atop one of the tors.

I gasped – suddenly I gulped the air in. I heard – saw – the boy gasp. He was breathing in too. And in that moment, the strangest and most frightening feeling possessed me: that I had become one with the boy, or the six children, or even the land itself. We were all one on that vast field, struggling to catch our last breath.

'Lucy!' John shouted again, from somewhere far behind me.

Then, before I could understand what had happened, the bushes rustled, the boy was up, and just as quickly he was gone.

Or at least I thought he was.

I remember, the sky was grey. No colour in it – the patterns only bands of grey and dull white. There was no sun to help me illuminate what I thought I had just seen, though I would never be able to un-see it. The boy had looked more like some sort of monstrous creature, a wild thing. But in another world, in a different time, he could have been any of us. He could have been me. He could have been John – or even Tom.

'Lucy,' John said.

He was close to me now, removed from that faraway place.

'How come you don't come when I call you, you naughty thing?'

He was holding, as I said, some sort of rock in his hand. A crude rock. But when he stopped to look into my eyes, he saw what I could not hide.

'Lucy,' he said, 'what is the matter?'

I breathed out. John was himself, and I was Lucy Braithwhite. The children we were meant to be. The children we had always been.

'A boy . . .' I said.

John looked about us, then at me, then around again.

'What boy?' he said.

But I could say nothing else. The rock in John's hand was the only thing that mattered. If I were to describe what I had seen to him, he would have admonished me for being 'fanciful'. He was like father in that way, even at that age, unaware of his own shadows – the ones that would eventually overtake him. I was silent. I said nothing. The wind blew, and we studied the rock in John's hand. The six children were still now, resolved to withstand the wind. We made our way back to the house, over the hills, and around the bogs, and down the slopes that could be gentle and kind. And whenever my brother progressed more than a few steps ahead of me, I would turn back to look – always looking.

XII

WE NEVER DID set a place at breakfast for Mr Rivers that morning, nor did John ever emerge from his room. Before the lunch hour, I went up myself to see John, only to find him in his dressing gown going over some papers on his desk. Poor Henry was still there, dead in his cage, and I called for Mr Jayne, but Mr Jayne did not come. John seemed unfazed by the loss, and did not appear as terrible as I expected. I will not say he looked cheerful, but he had at least felt well enough to rise and work. Well, what little work John could do, anyway.

I pulled aside the curtains to let more light into the room. Then I sat close to him, in one of the chairs near the desk.

'You did not feel well enough to come down?' I finally said.

'No,' John said.

He continued looking over the papers.

'Was the rest of your sleep sound, then?' I asked.

The question stopped him right there, and the paper he held trembled. He set the paper down, made a kind of fist, and looked up at me.

'Sound?' he said.

His eyes were dark – lined with red. He had a terrible, resentful look. I reached over to touch his hand, but he abruptly pulled himself away.

'It's horrible,' he said.

Then he went back to his piece of paper.

'John—' I began.

But he shot up his hand.

'Lucy,' he said. 'It is all too horrible, and I don't know what to make of it. These visions – hallucinations – they . . .'

'But I *do* know,' I said to him, gripping his hand with both of mine. 'I do know, John. And I do understand.'

He shook his head. He held my hand. His emotions were all dammed in.

'No!' he said.

Here he was, my brother, facing something he never expected to have to face. I suppose, for the first time, his innocence was being truly shattered. I looked into his eyes. He was a child all over again.

'It is all right, John,' I said. 'No harm will come to you. Not while I am here.'

A small tear escaped his eye. He bowed his head, but then lifted it and said:

'Even after father was gone, I knew that he was always with me. That his – going – was not some final departure. He was still everywhere, around me.'

'I know,' I said.

My brother would never escape that feeling.

'And I tried to live as best I could for him,' John said. 'The way he would have hoped for me to live. To accomplish all the things . . .'

John's hand was soft in mine, and we were very much together.

'But in the end,' he said. 'I've failed him. And now—'

'John!' I exclaimed. 'Do not speak of successes or fail-
ures. You are the man you were meant to be. Nothing more,
nothing less. We all have our burdens.'

'He—'

But before John could continue, Mr Jayne appeared. Mr
Rivers had arrived, and was waiting.

I would like to say that I was surprised by the announce-
ment, but I was not, for all morning that dreaded thought
had been in the back of my mind – that Mr Rivers could
show himself at any time, and that I would be forced to take
him up to see my brother. That I was with John, and in a
moment of intimacy with him in his room, only made the
arrival that much worse. John's mood changed, though. His
posture straightened, and he was quick to wipe his eyes. He
gave my hand a last squeeze and then, straightening his dressing gown, asked Mr Jayne to show our guest into the room.

This was, if I am remembering correctly, the first time Mr
Rivers had ever *begun* one of his visits in the room where
John slept. John had been in such a good state up until then
that he – we – had always received Mr Rivers in the drawing
room. Mr Jayne retreated. John and I waited some moments.
Then Mr Rivers came bounding in, delightful as ever.

'Rivers,' John said, 'you'll excuse my appearance. I had a
little bit of a turn last night.'

Mr Rivers looked at me, then back at John.

'I am sorry to hear it, sir,' Mr Rivers said, moving towards
us. 'I came as soon as I could. Your note seemed urgent,
and I was worried.'

He looked over at the window, strangely. He had not come
urgently. In fact he had not come for hours. What words, I
wondered, had my brother written to summon him?

Then Mr Rivers did something I had never seen him do. He lost that charming composure of his for the slightest moment, as his eyes moved away from the window and fell somewhere else.

'What happened to the bird?' he said.

He was moving towards Henry's cage now, his face shadowed with concern.

'Ah yes, poor Henry,' John said. 'Had an attack during the night. A good old soldier he was. With us our whole lives.'

But Mr Rivers did not respond, or even seem to hear John. His state had grown – I am not exactly sure how to describe it – but he appeared to have grown remote. He undid the cage's latch, reached his hand inside, gently lifted out Henry's carcass, and – well again, it is somewhat difficult to imagine him doing such a thing now, but he actually *cradled* the bird in his hand.

Then, with his other hand, Mr Rivers petted Henry's head.

'Such a beautiful creature,' he said.

I then saw something in Mr Rivers that I had never seen in him before: a child. Yes, it was very brief and out of character. But for that one moment even he could not disguise himself. Mr Rivers was, like us – like all of us – someone's child.

The thought disturbs me, even now. I was torn between loathing him and feeling for him.

Mr Rivers then turned towards us, holding Henry at a little distance.

'Rivers,' John said. 'Are you all right?'

Mr Rivers approached us – or me rather. He came straight to me with Henry in his hands. He set the bird in my lap, and we were all quiet for a moment. I held Henry. The poor creature would need to be buried. His beautiful eyes and feathers decomposing somewhere in the ground.

Then John said:

'Lucy, please leave us.'

I looked at my brother, who was glancing down at his papers. I looked at Mr Rivers. His eyes had been fixed upon me.

'Leave you?' I said.

'Yes,' John said.

I cannot say that Mr Rivers smiled, because I don't think he did. But something had transpired and I didn't know how it had happened. Mr Rivers wanted me to leave. Mr Rivers wanted *John* to want me to leave. And somehow, in those brief seconds following the transfer of Henry from his hands to mine, Mr Rivers had made it all come to be.

I felt myself growing hot.

'Yes, John, of course,' I said.

Then I rose, and rushed from the room. My cheeks, I knew, had flushed. The less Mr Rivers saw of me in such a state, the better. Not that he needed to see anything to *know*. For he already knew that I was both afraid and on my guard – that the world he was slowly constructing within our house was one in which I would ultimately be powerless. Yes, that was the crux of it. One could not trust anything he did.

I went downstairs to find Mr Jayne. He was polishing various pieces of silver and returning them to the sideboard. How comforting it was to see him in his place – simple and dependable Mr Jayne.

'Oh, miss,' he said, putting down his work and coming towards me to collect Henry. 'I'm so sorry, miss.'

He took Henry from my hands, and bowed his head.

'Poor old chap. I remember the day he came into the house. You and Mr Braithwhite were but little things. And you did not want him to be here in the worst way, miss. You were so scared of the poor creature. But you were such a little thing then.'

'Scared?' I said.

For I had been scared of many things as a girl, but never of Henry.

'Oh yes, miss,' Mr Jayne said. 'You don't remember?'

Just then, Susan entered the dining room as well. She saw Mr Jayne holding the dead bird, and brought her hands to her head.

'Oh, the injustice of it!' she cried out. 'There's never any relief!'

'Please take him,' I said. 'We'll want to do something nice for him.'

And I nodded them both out of the room.

'In the garden.'

Then Susan and Mr Jayne took Henry downstairs, a melancholy air following them as they went. But in that moment, for me, there was no time for mourning. My brother was with Mr Rivers, conducting his business, and I was eager for that business to conclude. I returned upstairs, and all was quiet. In the drawing room, I would wait.

The day was dull, the light was grey, and the bold patterns in the drawing room were forming into a storm. An hour passed – it might have been two – and I waited, John and Mr

Rivers deep in their business. Before everything had started to happen, I had tended to be pleased, excited even, that John and Mr Rivers were spending so much time together. But now, everything in the air around us had changed. The clouds had taken shape, and day by day, we were growing more and more unsafe in our own house.

There was an eerie stillness to the light that came in that afternoon, its greyness painting over everything as if with the thinnest layers of smoke. I walked about the room. I read. I straightened vases. I frequently looked out of the window to see if Mr Rivers's boy was still there. He wasn't. But then, after a moment, I noticed him crouching near our portico, like some camouflaged little creature, invisible at first. I had not spoken to the boy since the night he had delivered the letter, though I had often had the urge to do so. He was, to my consternation, as unpredictable as his master: sometimes he was there, and sometimes he was not.

My mind wandered again. How had Mr Rivers acquired the boy? Where had the boy come from, and where did he live now? Did he live with Mr Rivers, somewhere in the East End, or did he go home to some sort of family, and give a loving mother his wages? I looked down at him through the lace of the curtains. He was casually pacing back and forth now, guarding the horse, or our house, or some other thing of great importance. The poor urchin, with perhaps nothing else in life, must have possessed a heightened sense of his own small duties. He was almost a man. Where would he go in the world? I remembered the day I had first recognised him from the very spot where I was standing. How he had cowered before his unfeeling master, the man who could help make him – or ruin him.

Again, I do not know exactly how much time had passed, but as I was moving away from the window, I heard the latch of John's door. Then went the vision of a hurried Mr Rivers, briskly passing by the drawing room on his way to the stairs.

'Mr Rivers!' I called out.

The man returned. His figure filled the door frame, and he stood there looking at me with those ever-sparkling eyes.

'Miss Braithwhite,' he said.

'Mr Rivers, please . . .' I said.

I motioned for him to enter, and with the greatest air of deference, he obeyed and sat down.

'It seems your brother was very unwell last night,' he said.

'You know that he was,' I replied.

'Yes.'

'It is not the first time,' I said, 'but I think you know this too.'

'Yes.'

'It is always back and forth with him. It has been that way since he was young.'

'Yes,' Mr Rivers repeated, 'but this time it is different.'

He was horrid. Perhaps John had told him everything. After all, John said that he had been compelled to tell Mr Rivers things that he would later regret. There was no doubt in my mind that when the two of them were together, there were no boundaries between them, that the professional lines that should have separated them blurred into something else. I found it hard to look at him, but not because he was evil. That was the thing: in looking at him, *one could see no evil there*. He was cheerful, he was beautiful, he was the humblest and most devoted of servants. I questioned myself, for I could not understand it. Or perhaps it was just that I did not want to believe it.

'I am correct in saying so, aren't I?' he said.

'In saying what?' I said.

'That it is different this time.'

'Yes, Mr Rivers, you are correct about that,' I said.

'And why do you suppose that is?' he said.

He wanted me to say it. He was inviting me to confess it. I tore my eyes away from him. I had a horrible urge to scream.

'*Why?*' he pressed.

Then mother came into the room, and all the air in my lungs went out of me.

'Ah, Mr Rivers,' she said, moving closer to join us, 'you've arrived at last. We thought you might have come in the morning.'

'I was delayed, Mrs Braithwhite,' Mr Rivers replied. 'But I've just spent the past hour with Mr Braithwhite, and all is well. All is very well indeed.'

'I think last night was not good for him,' mother said.

'No,' Mr Rivers said, 'and it pains me that he often takes so ill.'

'It pains us all,' mother said, 'but in this house there have been many unkind nights. We live with them. Sometimes, it is hard to be strong.'

Mr Rivers looked about the room, assessing the chairs, the lamps, the card tables, as if all of those items were now his friends too, and would support him in whatever it was he was trying to do.

'We like to fancy ourselves strong,' he said. 'Safe and strong. But how delicate the balance is, how common that a mere colour – in a room, in the sky, or in a scrap of forgotten verse – should shake one's nerves to the core with the return of the subtlest memory.'

Mother softened even more at this poetry.

'Yes,' she said. 'It is all very precarious.'

There was some quiet between us. Was mother thinking him brilliant? Then Mr Rivers said:

'But your son is strong.'

'He is strong,' I agreed.

'He is strong,' mother affirmed.

But when she said it, everything in her voice revealed that she did not believe herself, and Mr Rivers perceived this. Mother and Mr Rivers could not have possibly been communicating, but there was a kind of communication there, an *entreaty* from mother. *Keep him safe*, she was saying. *Don't spoil him. Don't influence him. He is not of your world, and we need you to safeguard him. We need you to safeguard* all of us.

And of course Mr Rivers would have heard it. Not that it mattered.

Just then, Mr Jayne entered the room, bearing the most enormous vase filled with every kind of flower. There were roses and daisies and willow branches, I think, and long-faced yellow lilies – all of them as vibrant as they were out of season.

'Ah, thank you, Jayne,' Mr Rivers said.

I was confused. I looked at mother.

'Yes, thank you,' she said. 'How kind of you, Mr Rivers.'

'Miss Braithwhite,' Mr Rivers said, 'I hope these will help lessen the difficulties of your day, and remind you that I am here as a servant and a friend.'

Then he turned towards me with more deliberateness, as any flower turns towards the sun.

'I only want to be – your friend.'

The flowers screamed with colours so garish that I almost winced. I looked at mother, and at Mr Rivers, and suddenly the whole plan was clear before me. She had known the flowers were coming. Had John known about them too? Had this offering been the cause of Mr Rivers's delay? Had his boy been waiting all this time for the delivery?

How I had not seen it earlier was something that embarrassed me. All signs had been leading up to it, and I *should* have been smart enough to perceive them. For the same kinds of things had transpired long ago with Mr Carmichael, before Mr Carmichael changed his mind, and went away. Only back then, the match had been clear and well-suited, whereas this time it was quite different, and involved a kind of descent that was humiliating. Fool that I was, I had so vehemently taken up my post to protect my brother that I had ever carelessly abandoned any determination to protect myself. And all this time I had been thinking that Mr Rivers had come to take John, I was wrong. Mr Rivers had come to take everything.

Mother's behaviour was what was most shocking. My whole life I had known her to be *only* on her guard. But she had completely fallen – succumbed. Even her impenetrable snobbery would no longer protect me. Oh mother – how horrible to think back on it now. In those last weeks you became someone I could no longer trust!

Mr Rivers stood to go, and I stood with him, quiet, but inside my rage was mounting. Mother remained seated and held out her hand. Mr Rivers took it, and when he did so, a shudder moved through me.

'Thank you for coming, Mr Rivers,' mother said. 'I hope you will come again soon.'

My stomach turned. The whole thing was so awful.

Then, as I was leaving with him, mother called out:

'I'll rest again, Lucy.'

'Yes, mother,' I returned. 'I'll wake you before dinner.'

It was horrid.

Mr Rivers and I descended the staircase in silence and reached the front door. Thank goodness for Mr Jayne, who was moving about in the dining room. He came out to help Mr Rivers with his coat and his gloves, and stood there alongside of me, the only protection I felt I had. Mr Rivers held his own hat – he did not move forward to touch me. Mr Jayne opened the door for him, and Mr Rivers stepped through.

'Good afternoon, Miss Braithwhite,' he said, smiling.

He put on his hat.

'I hope that you will remember what I've said. I will come again soon.'

Behind him, on the pavement, the boy looked in at me with a fearful expression – he seemed to be saying something, wanting something, but no other intercourse between us was possible. As his master turned around, he quickly averted his gaze. Then Mr Jayne closed the door. The latch echoed as it clicked.

There was a pause, and finally I breathed.

'Are you all right, miss?' Mr Jayne said.

'Yes, Mr Jayne. Thank you.'

'A . . . nice gentleman, miss?' Mr Jayne said.

'Do you think so?' I asked.

One side of Mr Jayne's face moved – a barely perceptible twitch.

'A nice enough gentleman, miss.'

Mr Jayne would never reveal his true thoughts. Even under these circumstances, I could not expect him to do so.

'And he is fond of Mr Braithwhite,' Mr Jayne added. 'Mr Braithwhite has grown to trust him.'

'Yes,' I said. 'It seems that a great deal has developed between them.'

Mr Jayne nodded. He chewed his lip.

'You will watch over my brother for me, won't you, Mr Jayne?'

'Of course, miss,' Mr Jayne answered. 'It is the only thing I can do.'

There was a feeling between us – a feeling in the house that we both understood. Like Susan, like old Mrs Dawes downstairs, Mr Jayne had been through it all with us, from the beginning.

XIII

WE MOVED UNEASILY into November, the days grew shorter, and my brother did not improve. If there seems a great finality in those words, it's because there was: John was not going to recover. I have described how in the past John had had his bouts, some more serious than others, and how even with the worst of them there had always existed some possibility of revival. But as Mr Rivers had so meanly observed, there was something very different about what was happening this time. John's face, for practically his entire life, had been like a changing landscape, flitted over with shadows and sunshine that exchanged places throughout the day. But now the shadows had begun resting upon him longer and longer, and the sunshine, what I could glimpse of it, was transient. There had been moments – so many – when we had thought that John was truly growing stronger, and that the 'difference' this time was going to be the dawning of a new day for him. But all those good episodes, in those first days and weeks with Mr Rivers, had been nothing more than a deceptive prelude to the awful thing that was still coming. For, now I knew, there was a vampire in our midst – a bloodthirsty creature who had come to feed on my brother. On all of us.

The visions worsened, but not in the way that you might think. Because, you see, the phantoms that haunted my brother were not like any of the night prowlers that one reads about in macabre novels. For John had taken a turn, and so too had his companions, who would now make themselves known to him at any time of day or night. John slept – in the morning, in the afternoon, in the evening – to escape his nightmares, only to awaken to the very company he had been trying to evade. John had become Tom. He was my little brother all over again. Sometimes, on the walls, he saw nothing more than a curve or a branch – the bright green of an emerald forest, the verdant shapes in the twisted design. But somewhere in there, always hiding, always lurking, was the ghastly infection that grew stronger as it rested.

I searched – for anything in the patterns that would make me one with my brothers. But the more I strained, the more the shapes and colours distorted themselves into nothing. What was there? What tortured John? And what had tortured Tom? I understood that there was something, but I could never see for myself what it was.

Mr Rivers remained charming – to everyone else but me, that is. Well, I suppose that is not actually true, for Mr Jayne, I could tell, held his suspicions, as did Susan in her simple way. The Stapleton-Graces, too, had grown quite fond of Mr Rivers. That November they had been calling twice as often as they normally did, perhaps intentionally, knowing that John had grown quite ill, and that Mr Rivers would be coming around that much more.

There was one day – I'm remembering, I think, a day somewhere in the middle of November – when the Stapleton-Graces had come for a visit, but Mr Rivers was not there. Mother had been doing quite well in the days prior, but

John had not, and remained in his room. Mr Stapleton-Grace had gone in to see John, while mother and Mrs Stapleton-Grace and I remained in the drawing room. Mr Stapleton-Grace was not gone long – perhaps ten or fifteen minutes – when he returned, shaking his head, his expression troubled and morose.

'The poor lad,' he said. 'And he has been doing so well. It pains me to see another one of these downward turns.'

'He will improve again,' I said.

'He always does,' mother added.

It was important to give the Stapleton-Graces no more reasons to check in on us.

'The room is in such a state,' Mr Stapleton-Grace said.

'I know,' I said, 'but even in his condition, John insists on keeping track of everything.'

'Is that really possible?' Mr Stapleton-Grace questioned. 'With those mountains of papers piled up on his desk?'

'I do believe so,' I replied.

'And Rivers?' Mr Stapleton-Grace said. 'He goes in there? He understands the state of things?'

Mr Stapleton-Grace was making quite an issue, and once again I wanted him to leave.

'He understands everything quite perfectly,' I said.

We exchanged more words, and mother spoke profusely about Mr Rivers's loyalty to both the company and the family. She had her own motives, and he had his, and I now understood that they had formed some kind of alliance against me. But none of this was on the surface, and we continued to talk around Mr Rivers's 'loyalty' until there was a lull, during which I hoped the conversation might take some other turn.

But it didn't.

'You know,' Mr Stapleton-Grace continued, 'they are all quite fascinated by Rivers down at the club.'

Mother stiffened.

'*Mr Rivers*,' she said, 'is a member of your *club*?'

Mr Stapleton-Grace laughed.

'Oh no – of course not. He's just the talk of it. All the business around town is.'

'I see,' mother said.

Mr Stapleton-Grace leaned in his chair.

'They are quite fascinated by him,' he said, 'how a man from the west country could rise in the way that he has. And that whole business with Selby, which no one knows anything about directly, mind you, but the talk . . .'

'It's true,' mother said, 'Mr Rivers, being from one of our families in Devon, would not strike anyone as a candidate for the position he's assumed, but I think we can all agree that Mr Rivers is quite . . .'

She paused. I did not think I could bear one more 'extraordinary'.

'He's quite brilliant, Clarissa,' Mr Stapleton-Grace said.

'He is indeed,' mother agreed. 'Mr Rivers is quite brilliant.'

'What he's done with the business. It's absolutely astonishing. But some say—'

Mother frowned. I folded my hands.

'Some say,' I interrupted, 'that a man of his background could never accomplish what he has on his own.'

'It seems that he and John have formed the perfect partnership,' Mr Stapleton-Grace said. 'Mr Luckhurst trained the boy. But John, who has always been brilliant in his own

144

way, is the one who is allowing for all the progress. It's the only way it could be.'

The words were very strange. But they were not a surprise.

'I see that now,' Mr Stapleton-Grace said. 'Having seen all those papers.'

That the disorderliness of John's room, and the dishevelled heap of papers upon John's desk, had told Mr Stapleton-Grace so much, infuriated me greatly. It was not his business, and I wished that he hadn't made it so. But the truth was that Mr Stapleton-Grace was someone who drew his conclusions quickly, guided by his own snobbery, whatever the case might be. Men like him could never completely accept a man like Mr Rivers as the true heir to the secrets and workings of an establishment as mighty as Braithwhite & Company. Other men could occupy all sorts of positions, and run every aspect of the business from top to bottom, but in Mr Stapleton-Grace's mind a Braithwhite, and only a Braithwhite, was capable of understanding the deepest and most vital aspects of the company.

'John does do an immense amount of work,' mother said, 'even in his state.'

'I can see that,' Mr Stapleton-Grace said.

'Poor John, though,' Mrs Stapleton-Grace interjected. 'Perhaps he should not be working so hard.'

She paused, then added:

'In his state.'

'That is the problem,' Mr Stapleton-Grace said. 'Rivers needs John. He could not do any of what he does without him.'

The words struck me like the coldest splash of water on a burning face. I had actually never considered it. I had never considered the idea that, without John, Mr Rivers could not properly move any operation forward on his own. Mr Rivers was able to do everything that he did – everything – because John willingly gave him the power to do so.

It was astonishing that I had missed something so simple.

And of course, it followed that the only way Mr Rivers would be able to do anything on his own was if he were to become a Braithwhite – or rather, a member of the family – himself. And that's when it dawned on me that I had of course missed that too. I had missed the idea that bringing Mr Rivers into our family, through me, had become something that mother, and perhaps even John, deemed necessary for the good of the company. It did not matter that he was from the west country, nor that he was someone in our employ. In the end, it was the company, and not me, that mattered most.

How could I have been so foolish not to have seen it?

'He is sharp,' Mr Stapleton-Grace said. 'He is very, very sharp.'

'Yes,' Mrs Stapleton-Grace chorused, 'and I think his growing ever closer to the family could only be good for . . .'

I tightened.

'Well,' she said, 'for business.'

There it was then, out in the open. All of them conspiring against me. I wondered just how much they had all talked amongst each other already. Had Mr Rivers spoken plainly with John about asking for my hand? Had he talked privately with mother? Was this something already being gossiped about at the club?

My rage towards them was welling. I could have murdered them all.

I looked at mother, but she was not looking at me. Her eyes were darting. Then her eyelids drooped and, with trembling hands, she fell forward.

'Clarissa!' Mr Stapleton-Grace cried, as he rushed from his seat to catch her.

I leapt up and rang for Susan and Mr Jayne. Mr Stapleton-Grace gently pushed mother towards the back of the couch. Mother was breathing, softly, but her eyes were closed, and her neck was limp. She looked paler than usual, and her cheeks had sunk that much more.

'Mother,' I said. 'Mother, are you all right?'

She did not respond.

'I'll run round and fetch Dr Merrick,' Mr Stapleton-Grace said.

He left the room just as Susan was coming in.

'Some compresses, miss?' she said.

I nodded. Certainly we had dealt with mother fainting before, but usually there were warnings, and mother herself would often announce when something was coming on.

Mrs Stapleton-Grace sat next to mother and held her hand. There had been something odd about the fainting, and not just the suddenness of it. I had the awful feeling, somewhere deep within me, that *I* had brought it on with some strange transfer of my anger. My fury had heightened during the moments before it happened, with Mrs Stapleton-Grace talking about 'good business', and everyone surely understanding what that meant. Not only had I felt betrayed, but my anger was growing – growing around everyone's blindness to the increasing momentum that threatened our family. And yet, because I was the only one who could see it – who did see it – I could not blame them, or be angry with any of them. The only other person who might have understood my feelings was John, because he too had started to see things that no one else could see. But his visions were of a very different sort, and he was so infatuated with Mr Rivers that I held no hope that he would dependably take my side.

And so I had to face the truth that I was utterly alone.

Susan left and returned. Mr Jayne came in as well, but I dismissed him, asking him if he would please to go and check on my brother. I took the compress from Susan and began applying it to mother's eyes and forehead. Mother's skin was dry – papery almost – pulling away from itself, and accentuating her hollowness.

She did not stir. Moments passed. Then Mr Stapleton-Grace returned with Dr Merrick.

'How long has she been like this?' the doctor asked.

'Only these few minutes,' I said. 'Since Mr Stapleton-Grace went to get you.'

'And she has not moved?'

I shook my head.

Dr Merrick gently pried mother's eyes open with two of his fingers, touched the side of her neck, and held her wrist to feel her pulse. Then he reached into his bag for a bottle of salts, opened the bottle, and held it to mother's nose.

Mother winced. She moved her head. Slowly, she parted her eyes. She blinked, and looked about herself, confused.

Mrs Stapleton-Grace still held her hand.

'I'm sorry,' mother said. 'What . . .'

'You've had a spell, Clarissa,' Mrs Stapleton-Grace said. 'It's all right.'

Mother closed her eyes again and breathed. Then moved her other hand over Mrs Stapleton-Grace's. Dr Merrick felt mother's neck again, nodded, and drew himself away.

'Thank you for coming, Doctor,' mother said. 'I am sorry to have been such a bother.'

'It's quite all right,' Dr Merrick said. 'This will pass. Just be sure to get some rest, and take care not to exert yourself in the next few days.'

Dr Merrick closed his bag, and the Stapleton-Graces had the good sense to begin collecting themselves. I accompanied the three of them downstairs while Susan remained in the drawing room with mother. In the front hall, I thanked each of them for being there, especially Dr Merrick, who had come on such short notice. They all buttoned themselves up and proceeded out of the front door.

Then I saw, from my vantage point in the open doorway, a thing that made all my skin grow cold. It was the boy – Mr Rivers's boy – leaning behind the lamp post across the street. He was greedily taking in the whole scene, and as our guests descended our steps, his eyes locked with mine. I could not tell whether he were terrified, or trying to terrify me. I had caught him or he had caught me – both were the same. He was frozen. He gripped the post. Then he ran.

The vision of the boy stayed with me as I returned upstairs to mother. I could not help but think that his presence there had somehow contributed to what had happened. For everything surrounding Mr Rivers worked like some treacherous spell, and though the boy had merely been lingering in the street, all that he represented – the watchfulness, the invasiveness – might as well have been inside with us.

We got mother into her room, and there I remained with her for a while. She sat up in one of the chairs, slouching herself comfortably to one side against the cushions. Though the day was already fading, I drew most of the curtains. Even that light was too much for her though, and she kept her eyes closed.

The sun stole into the room with the impulsive naughtiness of a child, casting slices of light here and there upon the birds that flew across the paper. I thought of Henry, and wondered if only I had been more discerning, or had done something differently, I possibly could have saved him. I supposed, though I didn't know for sure, that Mr Rivers had been the one who had brought Henry into John's room. Mr Rivers had touched the cage. Mr Rivers had set the scene. I had been upstairs with mother and had abandoned my station.

Mother stirred.

'You are so good to me, Lucy,' she said.

I did not respond.

'It's not been fair for you,' she said.

'Not fair?' I replied.

'No,' mother said. 'It's not been fair for any of us, but it's been especially unfair for you.'

I was quiet. There was a bird above the dresser that I particularly detested. One came face to face with him whenever one opened the top drawer. And of course, he was repeated in many other places too. He was perched on a gnarled branch, surrounded by bright green leaves.

'I want . . .' mother began.

But then she paused and touched her forehead. The afternoon and the fainting – next would come the headache.

'Mother, don't speak,' I said.

'No,' she said. 'I must say it.'

She kept her eyes closed. She was weak.

'I want what is best for you, Lucy. I only want what is best for you. You deserve that, and when I am gone, and John, well . . .'

She paused again. I knew what she wanted to say, but I was not about to help her say it.

'I think he's come to save us,' mother said.

Then, she said it again:

'He's come to save us.'

'Mr Rivers,' I said.

'Yes,' mother said. 'Mr Rivers.'

The blindness. I was not about to respond. She couldn't see it. She could only see what she thought would be 'best'.

'I don't think you understand,' mother said.

That confused me.

'What do you mean?'

She was quiet again. The entire house was quiet. No one was stirring downstairs.

Mother breathed.

'Things must change,' she said. 'If they don't there will only be more sorrow. The company – our family. There has been such sorrow. He will change it all, Lucy. He will make it so that we can continue.'

She was not making sense.

'Change what, mother?'

She opened her eyes.

'The formulas,' she said.

'What on earth are you talking about?' I said.

'He will change them,' mother said. 'He will make things right.'

And then I saw where her mind was going – or had gone. She had been blinded by him, misinterpreted him somehow. She was thinking that he would make the formulas *better*.

'Mother,' I said, 'I don't think you are correct.'

But for the first time, for a mere second, I wondered.

'I am, Lucy,' she insisted. 'He will make them safe. He will make *all of us* safe.'

It was nonsense. I was growing impatient.

'Mother—' I said.

But she did not let me go on.

'You did not see what I saw,' she said. 'You were only a girl. Your father – he hated me going amongst the workers, in Devon. But I had to go. It was my duty to go. It was my atonement – for what had happened.'

'Mother,' I said, 'don't speak so. You will bring on the headache.'

'I saw the most horrible things,' she pressed on. 'Suffering that one should never have to cast one's eyes upon. The yellow fingernails, the ulcers, the lesions, the pocks that covered their skin! It was all coming from the mines – what we were extracting from the mines. We were doing it, Lucy. Us.'

'The conditions were never ideal,' I said. 'That much has always been known.'

Mother clutched at her chest.

'But the sin of it!' she exclaimed. 'Those poor people, and what they've suffered. What everyone's suffered.'

She breathed out again.

'And then there was Tom.'

I started, and suddenly my eyes burned and my throat tightened. Again, my shame overwhelms me as I write, for I did not want to hear it. I couldn't then.

'Mother,' I said coldly. 'We had nothing to do with what took Tom.'

With half-closed eyes she peered at me.

'We had everything to do with it,' she said.

I had but a moment to absorb the awful words, but I could only absorb so much. I am sorry for it.

'I cannot breathe,' mother said.

She had fallen a bit forward. I got up, leaned her back, and reached for another compress.

'No,' she said, motioning me away with her hand. 'Open the window for me. The air is so thick.'

'Mother, the cold—'

'Please!' she exclaimed.

'The cold air will bring on the headache. I cannot.'

She frowned and reached out to take the compress herself. The cloth looked as big as a mast sail in her tiny fingers. She dabbed her eyebrows, and then pressed the cloth against her eyes. It was twilight. The sky was turning pink. The birds were twisting in the shifting light. I myself was starting to feel that I could not breathe. I wanted mother to go to sleep, and I wanted to get myself out of the room.

'You will not come down to dinner, I think,' I said.

'I think not,' she whispered.

'I will bring it up then.'

'No, nothing – please,' she said. 'I will sleep, and I will be better in the morning.'

So I left her, and was glad to.

There was an awful, inexorable inevitability to everything that was happening, which, strangely, acted as a kind of misplaced apology. A terrible idea was beginning to haunt me – that nothing about our family could ever change. That we would never have a choice. That we would forever be the same, never different.

But the dangers were mounting, and I had no time for apologies. I shut my eyes. I needed to keep going.

XIV

NEITHER MOTHER NOR John came down for breakfast the next morning. And for the rest of that day, they both remained in their rooms. Astonishingly, John got himself out of bed to work after lunchtime, and when I went in to bring him his dinner, there he was at his desk, still working. Something else strange had happened with regard to John's manner around this time: he was now, whenever I entered, in some kind of other world with his papers. He had energy, even ferocity, and displayed exuberance as he sat there scribbling. I cannot say that the work made him better – I would not let myself be misguided in that direction – but the return of his limited vigour when he engaged with his papers was, in the most unexpected way, oddly medicinal.

If there was any kind of cure for John it was that: a place of importance, and a position that allowed him to believe he had an effect, even if that place and position left him visibly strained. Of course, the work ran contrary to what any of the doctors prescribed for him, since Dr Merrick and everyone else insisted that he get more rest. We had been dealing with the doctors for years though, and really, I did not trust them. I never did – even though I would eventually be forced to reconsider all of their warnings. At the time, to my mind, their presence was more a palliative than anything, and one needed to weigh whatever they said against everything else one believed. If John was sick, it was because of what he had inherited, and no doctor, no matter how wise he might seem, was going to change my brother's course.

Two or three more days passed, and John and mother eventually emerged, though neither of them felt strong enough to come all the way down to dinner. They took their meals in their own rooms, and during the day we congregated in the drawing room, while John intermittently attended to his work and mother took frequent naps. Mr Rivers visited – that never changed – and voiced great concern over mother's condition.

'You must watch,' he said to mother, glaring. 'Every step you take now must be a careful one.'

'Oh, Mr Rivers,' mother replied, weakly, 'I thank you for your concern, but a woman of my age, well, these things—'

'You are an all-too-important link in the chain of this family,' he said. 'And the company. That link must remain strong as we continue.'

Mother acknowledged his words with a nod. Her discernment was all gone now – sacrificed to the belief in some ideal outcome she had dreamed up. It was shocking to me, the way she had completely given herself over. But now that I think back on it, perhaps I'm being too unkind. What choice did she have in the matter? What other outcome could she conceive? He was beguiling, and carried us only good news about the business. Mother wanted what was 'best'. What choice did any of us have?

Whatever the case, Mr Rivers remained on course, and brought me gifts: an inlaid hand mirror one week, a padlock pendant bracelet the next. When mother and John and

I were in the drawing room with him, we were all three his prisoners, but I felt that I especially had been singled out as his worst ward. My knowledge and understanding of him meant that I could not be let out of sight, that everything I did and said needed to be treated with suspicion, and that my efforts to undermine him, whatever they were, required a constant check. What was miraculous, though not surprising, was that, throughout all this, Mr Rivers was able to maintain all the charm and delightfulness that characterised him when we had first met. It was strange: the more he visited, the more oppressed I felt by him, and yet at the very same time, mother, John, and the Stapleton-Graces, only became more mesmerised by him, and what he was doing for us, and the company.

And then there was the marriage, for that's where this was going. No one breathed a word about it – even mother, when we were alone – but it was everywhere, muted but radiant, like an audacious background colour in one of our papers. Had I suggested even the slightest protest to the idea, my judgement would have been questioned, any reservation stamped out. Mr Rivers was 'very sharp'. Mr Rivers was exceptional. Mr Rivers was the very future of Braithwhite & Company. A woman like me would only be lucky to have him, they whispered. His coming into the family would result in profit all around.

The thought of the whole thing was revolting.

Had anyone, except for me, I wondered, stopped to think about what all of it might mean? How such a pairing, rather than sealing the cracks in our foundation, would actually disrupt and even demolish everything that was holding us firm? Would Mr Rivers come into the house? Would he somehow take it? Or would he take me somewhere else, far away from mother and John? Perhaps he would simply set me up in apartments in Camden Town, close enough to keep an eye on me, but far enough away for him to control everything. He would separate me from what I loved. He would separate me from John. And then he would finally be in a position to do whatever he wanted.

These things could not happen.

They could *never* happen.

I needed to think. Would my own plan come? I had very little time.

And then, the first fragments of the plan did begin to appear, quite randomly one day, as these things often do. Mr Rivers had spent the good part of the afternoon at the house, going over business with John in his room. When he left, I watched through the lace curtain of the drawing room, my face hidden from view, though nothing was ever hidden from Mr Rivers.

'It's such good news, isn't it?' mother said.

I turned from the window.

'Yes,' I said thoughtlessly.

'I told you,' mother said.

I knew what she meant, but I did not want to hear it.

'I told you,' she repeated, 'that he had come to save us.'

'The returns are very good, mother. That much is true.'

Though again, I did not quite believe anything Mr Rivers said at that point.

'We must trust in him,' mother said.

Only a fool would trust the devil, I thought.

And at last, after all this time, mother sensed that I was not in agreement with her.

'Lucy, my dear . . .' she said.

I looked at her.

'You do not trust him?'

I waited a moment. I needed to be careful. Mother could upset everything if the wrong thoughts entered her head.

'I do not know whom or what to trust these days,' I answered. 'Things are never as they seem.'

Mother worried her hands.

'There is danger,' I added. 'You know this.'

She did know it. Our family had not been a stranger to the surrounding danger – forces pushing in upon us, over which we had no control. Father had fought against this, and his father before him, and Mr Luckhurst, and everyone else whose mission it was to protect our family. And I had played a part in that protection in my own way, as did mother, strange as our little roles in the grander scheme had been.

But now the danger wasn't only surrounding us from the outside. The worst threat was coming from within.

'He isn't family,' I said.

Mother looked both confused and stunned because, for one, I had never said anything so bold-faced about Mr Rivers, and for two, she must have realised that I was right.

'No,' she said simply.

There was some quiet between us.

'But he has been so *good* for John,' she finally said.

I did not reply.

'And for you too, Lucy.'

Mother needed there to be something good, for her sake, not for mine. For my own part, I had been asleep, but now I was awake.

'Mother,' I said, 'I must tell you, I will not—'

But mother threw up her hand.

'We must stay the course, Lucy,' she said. 'That is our duty.'

I remembered father's words – his cold and deliberate words. *Your duty is always to me, Lucy. To your father, and to the company. And after I am gone, it will be to your brothers, and the company.* There was no room for discussion. Indeed, there never was with father. And now mother was invoking him, only with that helpless air she wore so well.

She left me, and I was relieved when she retired. I was angry at her – at the servility she had never allowed me to question. I walked about the drawing room. I picked up Mr Donne. Then I tried Mr Spenser, but I simply could not concentrate. I cannot remember how long I remained there, but the time could not have been great. The day was cloudy and the cold crept in. One could only warm oneself if one were immediately by the fire.

Then I saw him. I would have missed him if I had not been at one of the north-facing windows, looking out not over our front, but over Weymouth Street instead. What caused me to be at that window at that very moment, I cannot say, but when I saw him lingering inside the threshold of our back gate, I knew that some force greater than myself had placed me there.

I ran out of the drawing room and raced down the stairs. Then further down into the kitchen and out the back door. He could not see me coming, of course, as the gate door was solid, and I made sure that, even in my haste, my movements were as silent and as careful as possible.

I approached the gate. He was still on the other side – I knew.

Then, with as much speed as I had in me, I undid the latch and threw the door open, just in time to catch a glimpse of the last fragments of his vanishing coat.

I leapt out onto the walkway.

'Stop!' I shouted.

But he did not stop.

'I've seen you!' I yelled. 'And I shall tell your master!'

This, I knew, would move the terrified culprit to stop, and he did. He was but part-way up the street. He stood there still, unsure of whether or not to continue.

'Boy!' I said. 'Do not run.'

He turned to face me, a deer stopped in mid-flight. I walked up to him, slowly. He was still poised to flee. He was a handsome young man, though his face was terribly filthy. And he was taller than I remembered, though not the height he would ultimately reach.

'What were you doing there, lingering about my gate?' I said.

'Please, miss—' he began.

He still wore the last looks of a child.

'Well?' I said.

'Nothing, miss,' he said. 'Please, miss—'

'Come with me,' I said grabbing the shoulder of his dirty coat. 'You shall come with me at once or your master shall hear what I have to say.'

'Oh no, miss,' he said, resisting. 'I can't.'

I tried to soften my gaze and locked eyes with his.

'You shall come with me,' I said. 'And everything shall be all right.'

Then he looked all around him, as if anticipating the beast to pounce. We were, after all, in the middle of the walkway, and though there were no other persons about, there was no telling who could be watching.

I tightened my grip on him.

'If you run, boy, you shall drag me. And then I will be forced to scream.'

He chewed his bottom lip.

'It will be all right,' I repeated. 'I promise you.'

And then the boy changed. His face sagged, his shoulders softened. I do believe that, up until that moment, he may never have heard any kind words of reassurance. I led him back through our gate, maintaining my hold on him all the while, and released him at the kitchen door, where I motioned him inside. Mrs Dawes was in there, chopping her parsnips. I sat the boy down at one of the tables and asked Mrs Dawes to leave.

On the counter, the puff pastry shells that Mrs Dawes had baked for that evening lay cooling – a dozen or so, assembled close together.

'What's your name, boy?' I said.

I went to the ice-box and took out the custard.

'Rob, miss,' he said.

'Well, Rob,' I said. 'You must be hungry. Boys of your age are always hungry.'

I pried the top from one of the pastries, filled the thing with custard, and sprinkled it generously with powdered sugar. Then I centred it on a small plate and placed the plate before him.

He looked at it, looked at me; looked back at the dessert, then looked at me again.

'Go on, Rob,' I said. 'It's for you.'

His eyes widened.

'Oh, I can't, miss.'

'And why not?'

'Because, miss – I just can't.'

I frowned.

'And why on earth not?' I asked again. 'I've made it just for you. If you don't eat it, you shall insult me.'

He hesitated longer, but I stared him down. Then at last, a dirty hand emerged from beneath the table, and moved forward.

'Ah, no, Rob!' I cried. 'I'm sorry – I didn't realise.'

I grabbed his sleeve, lifted him up, and guided him towards the sink.

'Wash,' I said.

And I handed him the soap. He lathered and scrubbed as I ladled some water out over his hands.

'Your master is such a meticulous man,' I said. 'I am surprised he lets you go about so.'

'Well, miss,' Rob said. 'He doesn't.'

'No? Then what's this?'

'He is very particular,' Rob said, 'always telling me to clean myself up. Only today . . .'

I handed him one of Mrs Dawes's clean towels.

'Only today what, Rob?'

'Only today,' the boy stammered, 'I fell into the street, and I haven't had the chance—'

'And why did you fall?'

The boy did not answer.

'Did someone push you?' I asked.

Still he did not reply.

'Your master pushed you.'

The boy looked down.

'No, miss,' he said.

'Why did your master push you, Rob?'

He shifted his feet, his clean hand resting on the edge of the sink.

'I was late,' he finally said, 'coming back with some papers.'

I took the damp towel with which he had dried his hands, and wiped some of the grime away from his forehead and his cheeks.

'You are a very handsome boy,' I said.

'Thank you, miss.'

'And now you must eat.'

We returned to the table, and Rob took a bite of the pastry. Then, he devoured the rest of it in only three or four more bites. He ate ravenously, but there was something more there than hunger. I tried to engage with him, but he would not meet my eyes.

When he was finished, two small lines of custard marked the corners of his mouth. I wiped them. Then I rose, assembled another pastry, and gave it to him.

'Oh, thank you, miss,' he said. 'You are very kind.'

A bit brighter this time, and a careful glance at me as he spoke. The little informant might indeed come around. He moved a finger towards the edge of the pastry, took a swipe at the custard, and ate it.

'Do you know who I am, Rob?' I said.

The boy nodded.

'Well, who am I then?'

'You are Miss Braithwhite,' he said.

'That's right,' I said. 'And who is Miss Braithwhite?'

'She is the mistress of this house,' he said.

'And what is this house, Rob?'

'This is a great house, miss. The house of Braithwhite & Company.'

'That's right. And as the mistress of this great house – the house of Braithwhite & Company – do you think that I am good or bad?'

'Oh! You are good, miss!'

'Are you sure, Rob?'

'Well, yes, miss. I know you are.'

He was looking at me now. He wanted to please me. He did not want me to dislike him.

'And how do you know, Rob?'

The boy paused.

'I know, miss. A cove knows.'

Indeed, the boy knew – a great many things. I could only imagine how long he had been spying on our family. And then I realised, he was in the kitchen. I had myself, of my own volition, brought him into the kitchen. And so now he would be able to return to his master and inform him about the details of another one of our entrances.

And yet, as this boy sat there before me, he could not disguise the sweetness that characterised him. How he had come to be with Mr Rivers, and how that man had somehow failed to ruin him, was a mystery.

Most of all, Rob was careful.

'He cannot find out I was here, miss,' he said.

'Your master shall find out nothing,' I said. 'For certainly I shall never tell him. Will you?'

Rob shook his head.

'You have done much on your own, haven't you, Rob?' I said. 'You've been alone. There have been challenges. You've had to find your own way.'

Again, he studied his plate.

'Yes, miss,' he said at last. 'A cove does what he can.'

'Ah,' I said, 'well that makes two of us then, Rob. You don't realise, but we are very much alike.'

There was still a spot of grime on one of his cheeks, and I wiped that away now too.

'Rob,' I said, 'we are going to be friends.'

He looked at me.

'And so, as friends, you must tell me, why do you linger about my house so?'

He thought for a moment. He was very deliberate.

'It is not so much the house, miss,' he said, 'as it is I watch the neighbourhood.'

'What do you mean, the neighbourhood?' I said.

'The doctors, miss. Their comings and goings.'

'You watch the doctors?'

Rob nodded.

'And why is that?' I asked.

'I don't know, miss.'

'You don't know why your master has you watch the doctors?'

'No, miss. I only know that he likes to know where they go.'

He bit down on his lip – a habit of his, I could now see. He had said much more than he had ever intended to say, and the extent of his transparency frightened him.

'Oh please, miss—' he pleaded again.

'And what of this house?' I pursued. 'Does your master like to know who comes and goes here too?'

He looked at me, silent.

'Tell me, Rob,' I said.

'Well . . .' he struggled.

I waited.

'Yes, miss.'

'And – what do you tell him?'

'Well,' he said, after another pause, 'the truth is there is not much to tell.'

He was right. He could watch, but there wasn't much to tell. We received hardly any guests, our days were invariably the same, and Susan was usually the only one to leave the house. What Mr Rivers wanted to know, beyond what he knew already, I could not imagine. But then again, Mr Rivers was determined to learn everything, no matter how insignificant a thing might be.

The boy ate his second pastry and I offered him a third, but he genuinely refused it, having stuffed himself quite full. There were more questions that I wanted to ask him. Where did Mr Rivers live exactly? Did Rob live with him, or in some other place? With whom else did Mr Rivers keep company? Was he wicked? Were there other houses or people whom he watched?

But I refrained. I did not want to make the boy even more uncomfortable. He had already compromised himself by revealing the few things that he had told me.

'You are very good, Rob,' I said. 'And you shall come to me when you need me. You must perform your duties for your master, whatever they are, but here you shall always find comfort.'

His mouth moved. It was not a smile, but something like one.

'Thank you, miss,' he said. 'But I can't. And please, miss, if he ever finds out—'

'He shan't, Rob,' I said. 'You just remember what I'm telling you. In this house, you may find comfort when you need it – with me.'

I led him back out into the garden, unlatched the gate, and passed him through.

'I'm much obliged, miss,' he said.

Then he trotted along at a quickened pace towards Harley Street, turned a corner, and disappeared. He was off to watch the doctors, or some other unsuspecting persons whose lives might one day prove to be of interest to his master.

XV

MORE DAYS PASSED, and there was a great deal of correspondence back and forth from the office, but we did not see Mr Rivers. When, after some time, I asked John why Mr Rivers hadn't come, John said that Mr Rivers had been called to Devon on some matter of urgency. He would be back shortly, John said, and in the meantime I should be thinking of something special to prepare for him upon his return – perhaps quail or game hen.

'And we do know that Mr Rivers so enjoys the almond cake too,' mother added.

There simply was no end to the professed admiration for him. It infuriated me, especially since I felt powerless to counter it. But I would do what I needed to do, and play whatever part I needed to play. I would bide whatever time I might have, until the intruder revealed some weakness.

Mr Rivers did return, and soon after came to dinner. And when he arrived that evening and watched very carefully how the front door closed, it struck me all at once that he was trying to master the house, and had probably been doing so all along. Every window, every door, every keyhole, every latch – he wanted mastery over all of them, to understand thoroughly how they functioned. Rob had not said as much when he had admitted to his master's interests, but the motive was implicit: when were doors opened, when were windows closed, and when might any of them be locked or unlocked? It was not enough for Mr Rivers to have access to the daily business of our house. For some reason, he wanted to understand everything about getting in and getting out of it.

I was worried that I had been caught – that Mr Rivers might have seen me observing him – but John was coming down the stairs just then, and had called to him, and got his attention. Poor John, he was not well that evening, but was trying to look as smart as he could. With Mr Jayne's help, he had attempted to dress beautifully, but given his condition there was only so much he could do. Mr Rivers rarely revealed any kind of surprise in his expression, unless, of course, such revelation could benefit him somehow; but he must have been surprised at the sight of John that night, because really John did look frightful. My poor brother – his eyes had sunk deeper than they ever had, and any blood that had been colouring his cheeks was now gone. He walked slowly because he was weak, with feet made of granite. A different creature from the vigorous boy I remember running so freely over the hills.

They shook hands, John smiled, and Mr Rivers looked concerned.

'Are you sure you are feeling well enough to dine this evening, Mr Braithwhite?'

'Of course I am!' John answered. 'We have missed you these few days.'

We ate. The chatter was pleasant enough, and Mr Rivers told us of the closing of one of the mine shafts in Devon. All through the dinner I could not help but think of Rob watching from somewhere outside. What motions was he noting, what lights in upstairs windows did he observe?

What details would his master demand of him when they met again in the street?

Of course, no one else was thinking about any of these things. Mother and John were too delighted with Mr Rivers's company to suspect that he offered anything other than kindness and charity. Then, just as dessert was arriving, his chivalry, to my great annoyance, leapt forward one more step.

'Mr Braithwhite,' he said, 'I think perhaps you should retire.'

Mother and I looked at Mr Rivers, then turned to John. My brother had indeed been growing paler all evening. He looked disappointed, sad. Then said:

'Why so, Rivers?'

And then Mr Rivers did the most extraordinary thing. He stood up from the table, walked over to John, and gently, very gently, placed his hand on the back of my brother's neck.

'You are warm,' Mr Rivers said. 'Too warm. You should probably not have come down. Miss Braithwhite, I think you'll agree?'

I met eyes with him. His eyes were clear. They shined at me, though they said nothing.

'Yes,' I replied. 'You are correct, Mr Rivers.'

'He was insistent,' mother said. 'I told him that we would have been happy to entertain you, but he is stubborn, and he would not listen.'

'I wanted to be here for your return,' John said.

Mr Rivers's hand was still resting on my brother. Drawing more life out of him, I thought.

'I do not need to be here,' Mr Rivers said. 'Ring for Mr Jayne, and I shall be on my way.'

I did as I was instructed, and soon Mr Jayne arrived to take John upstairs. Mr Rivers had managed to usurp my place again. Oh, the man was generous!

Mother retired as well, and I accompanied Mr Rivers to the front door. My blood was boiling and I wanted to claw at him. To scratch out those brilliant eyes that were always taunting me so.

'Miss Braithwhite,' he said, beginning to fasten his coat, 'thank you for a lovely evening. You are always so considerate, and these evenings with you are my great joy. But I think I should stay away for a few more days. We do not want to be tempting your brother.'

There was a hint of something sinister in his smile, but it was nothing I could precisely identify.

'What do you mean by having your boy watch this house?' I blurted out. 'You can't think I haven't seen him. Is it your hobby to spy on your employers?'

And as soon as I said the words I was winded by my own regret. For Mr Rivers's smile moved not an inch. The devil had lured me in, and I had stupidly seized his bait.

'Miss Braithwhite,' he said, 'have I done something to offend you?'

I did not answer him, but only stared back at him, breathing heavily.

'I feel you are displeased with me,' he said.

The man, with his games. He was going to drive me mad.

'What is your purpose,' I insisted, 'keeping spies about this house?'

Then his smile did move, into an expression of absolute pleasure.

'My *employers*,' he emphasised, 'are my greatest concern.'

He picked up his hat and his gloves from the table.

'In fact,' he added, 'they are my *only* concern.'

'I appreciate that, Mr Rivers,' I said.

But he knew that I did not mean it.

'Did you enjoy him, then?'

'Pardon?' I said.

'Did you enjoy him?'

'Enjoy who?'

'My boy,' he said. 'Did you enjoy talking to Rob, the day before I left?'

He knew. He had discovered us. Poor Rob – I had condemned him! I could only imagine what the boy must have suffered since the last time I had seen him.

'You think that I do not know,' Mr Rivers said, 'but I do.'

My throat tightened.

'Know what, Mr Rivers?'

'That you need protection,' he said. 'I know you do not like to hear it. In fact, I know it is one of the most difficult things for you to hear. But what use am I to this family if I cannot be completely honest? Yes, Miss Braithwhite, you, and your brother, and your mother need protection. You always have. The company itself cannot protect you. For that, you need a friend.'

Oh, he was patronising. This boy from the country. How had he come to claim this place here before me?

Then I said exactly what he expected me to say:

'We have done quite well without anyone's protection.'

But he would not let me be.

'Miss Braithwhite,' he said, 'you know that isn't true.'

The insolence of the man. What could he possibly understand?

Then he narrowed his eyes, and peered into me.

'Have you any idea,' he said, 'of how many people hate us?'

'Hate us?' I said.

The words were a shock, though they shouldn't have been.

'The company,' he said. 'The family.'

'I'm sure I don't know what you mean, Mr Rivers.'

'You know exactly what I mean,' he said.

The insolence. The presumption.

'Forgive me, Mr Rivers,' I said pleasantly, 'but I feel you are being impudent, and I shall tell my brother of your impudence, as soon as he is well enough to hear of it.'

'You will do nothing of the kind,' Mr Rivers decided. 'You will not disturb anything that's going about here. I am the best thing that has ever come along for your brother, and you know this.'

He stared straight into me as he said it, daring me to contradict him. I would not. In his eyes I saw that I could not win — at least not then. But in that wild, glistening gaze of his I saw something else as well. He had said that people hated 'us', including himself in the collective. Ah, there it was then: the belief that was his singular weakness. As much as he despised us, he wanted to be part of us. Revealing that to me so plainly was the only mistake he ever made.

But I couldn't let him know this. If he ever realised I had discovered him, there would be an end to everything.

'You are right, Mr Rivers,' I said, softening. 'In so many ways my brother is better now than when you first found him.'

'You flatter me,' he said.

'I do not. We both know that it is true.'

He left. He could have gone in any number of directions, but he had chosen to focus on *my* greatest weakness – my love for my brother. But what this devil failed to understand was that my greatest weakness was also my greatest strength. Perhaps he thought me no more scheming than a lioness protecting her cubs – that what I did for my brother I did out of some sort of natural instinct, and that my maternal impulses cancelled my ability to see anything beyond what was right in front of me. But I could be scheming. I could plan too. And though I did not know yet exactly what my plan would be, I sensed that the plan was forming, and that it would reveal itself quite soon.

XVI

I CALMED MYSELF. Susan and Mr Jayne had retreated downstairs to the kitchen. I turned down the lamps and went back upstairs. The evening was over. The house was quiet again.

I looked into the drawing room and turned down the lamps in there too. Only hours before, we had all been in there together, conversing under the illusion of happiness. Mr Rivers had returned and John had been so delighted, as was mother, who, whether charade or no, continued to insist on brightening in our manager's company. All delight for me was gone, though – happiness no longer possible. The war was advancing, and my only delight, if one can even call it that, was to be found in preparing myself for the battle that was coming.

I retired to my own room and, to ease my mind, opened Mr Coleridge. *'Twas right, said they, such birds to slay . . . That bring the fog and mist.* I thought back. How long it had taken before mother had finally ordered the paper to be removed from my room. I had begged her. I had pleaded. I had cried and screamed. But it was not until one of the doctors – the dreadful doctors – had made the suggestion that she had relented. I looked at the light from the lamp on my walls. The light was soothing – plain – lacking all complication of pattern. Just a warm glow with no outline, a gentle illumination without shape.

I tired. The two candles on the mantel were guttering, but I was already too lethargic to bother to extinguish them. My book was in my lap. I had often fallen asleep thus. Ever since John's torments had begun, retiring to my own bed had grown more difficult.

I did not dream that night. All around me was dark and quiet. But then, from somewhere – how much later I could not say – the shriek cried out. I shook myself from slumber. The sound had not been a dream. I put down my book and waited. The sound would come again.

The candles had extinguished and the lamp was very low. My walls, a dark pink, breathed with weighty colour through their lustre.

Then I heard it – not a shriek this time, but a kind of muffled moan, as if the shriek had been smothered, its desperation reduced against its will. The sound echoed out in the hall, out in the space beyond my door. A horrible sound. A muffled sound, no less dreadful because it was not loud.

I threw on my robe and raced down the stairs. The sound could only be coming from John's room.

But no sooner had I reached the landing below when I was stopped, for I heard the terrible cry again, louder this time, coming from somewhere above me. I looked at John's door, then looked up the stairs. Was I being deceived? Had I rushed down to John's room, only to be recalled again by whatever was behind me?

My hand was on the banister. I was frozen. I did not move. *John . . . did you need me?*

Then, through the darkness, the awful cry rang out again. Unquestionably, the sound had come from somewhere above.

I made my way back up the stairs. All was silent now. The lamp in the hall was very low, and the shadows on the walls were mountains. I listened. Nothing screamed, and the walls were silent. I was alone there, all alone, standing again before my open door. Mother was in her room, John in his. Mrs Dawes and Mr Jayne in their rooms down below. Susan upstairs on the third floor, the nurseries empty –

Then it dawned on me. Upstairs. The sound had come from upstairs. It must have. That's why the sound had been muffled and remote.

Ah yes . . . now I understood.

It was strange, the way I thought about my younger brother, because my memories of him were both vivid and incomplete. The vivid ones – the ones that stuck to me like fabric on my body – were the most horrific, because of course I was the only one with him when he died. How he gasped for air as he stared with unblinking eyes at the distorted shapes that crawled before him. How with every pant he seemed to be inhaling more of their poison. For that's what they did to him – those faces, those children. They terrified him so much that on that night he could not catch his breath. And I, like a fool, lost my wits, and began to struggle too. I could not control it. I did not know what was happening. I could not see them. But somehow Tom and I had become one, and I felt that the same thing was trying to take us.

Even through his irregular panting, though, my little brother managed to speak to me. Those words – those last little words that escaped from his mouth, before he swallowed his last breath.

'Lucy,' he said, 'what is the matter?'

They were so simple, so much like him. My love, my dear little brother. And I held him, ever so tightly, because I did not know the answer. What could I tell him? What comfort could I bring? What words could I possibly have uttered that might have saved him?

'What is the matter?'

I hated them.

The moan came again, soft and distinct. The sound, unmistakable this time, stopped me as I was about to ascend. I turned my head and watched mother's door. The sound came again. It was mother.

Suddenly, another picture flashed before me. A vision from long ago – of mother fallen at her bedside, groaning. I could see her very clearly, in her mourning, the lights dim. It was right after Tom's funeral and we were still down in Devon – the last time that we would all be there together as a family. The soft muffles of her cries then were unlike anything one hears on this earth. Neither person nor sheep torn apart in the black of night could have made such horrible sounds.

Mother moaned again, and I burst into her room. It was no surprise to me that she was out of bed, collapsed on the floor. Her hair was down – long and grey, thick and tangled as a mass of wool. The sound leapt from her throat once more as I came in.

I rushed over to her.

'Mother,' I said, lifting her. 'Into bed.'

She was light – a broken bird, barely able to stand on her feet.

'You must get back into bed,' I said.

She wobbled, she folded. I managed to settle her on her mattress. Then I leaned her back, lifted her feet, and tucked her small body into the covers.

She heaved for some moments, but then her breathing calmed. She was crying. On the floor, there was the spilled vial of white powder.

I picked it up.

'What is this?' I said.

She looked at what I held. Her lids were heavy. Quivering and squinted.

She breathed.

'Mother,' I repeated.

'From Dr Merrick,' she said.

I put my nose to the vial. There was no scent.

'Dr Merrick,' I stated.

'From Dr Merrick. To help with . . .'

She breathed in and out again. Her hands on the covers mere bones.

'To help with what, mother?' I said.

'To help . . .'

But she would not finish. Even she realised that saying it out loud would sound as absurd and preposterous as the ideas of the doctors. To take poison, bit by bit by bit, as some sort of means of protecting yourself from it. Such nonsense. She did not know what she was doing. Only later would I think that perhaps she did.

'When did he give this to you?' I said.

'Long ago,' she whispered.

'How long?'

'I don't know,' she said. 'Some months.'

'You have been taking arsenic for some months!'

She swallowed.

'And why did you never tell me?'

'Because I knew it would upset you,' she said. 'I know you do not like to hear it.'

'How could you not tell me this?'

I was furious.

'How could you do this?'

But there was no point in scolding her. She had done what she had done. And for all I knew she was bending the truth too. Or worse, she was lying, and the arsenic had not in fact come from the doctor.

There was a kind of gurgling to her breathing, and I noticed that her lips were inflamed. There were tears in her eyes, though they came from no emotion.

'It is all coming to be,' she said.

'Quiet, mother,' I said.

And I poured some water.

'It is all coming to be,' she repeated.

I tried to hold the glass to her lips, but she motioned it away. Then she moved her head back on the pillow, her neck arched, the flesh of her neck stretched like canvas.

'*One child dead and one child living . . .*' she whispered.

No, no, mother. No –

Then she repeated it:

'*One child dead and one child living.*'

I waited. I prayed that she would not go on. There was a second line to the verse, but she did not say it. The infernal words of the old beggar woman in Tavistock.

'Do you remember?' mother said.

'Please, mother.'

'Do you remember her, Lucy?'

Now she moved her hand towards mine, and she took it, and held me softly.

'*One child dead and one child living; all children dead and no forgiving.*'

That woman – that horrible old woman in the square. I was terrified of her, hunched over like a goblin, dressed in rags. She was always begging, a wrinkled arm sticking out from her dirty shawl. She was covered with sores. No one knew who she was.

'You remember her,' mother said. 'How could you not? She called out to us that day – after the accident.'

'Mother, don't speak of it.'

'I remember it, Lucy. The sun was shining. There was no gloom in the square, though death had taken so many. Death was all around, but the sun was shining on us. I walked you through the square. You wore a lovely white dress that Mrs Dawes had made for you. There was a green bow on the front of it, a small and delicate ribbon around the waist. Do you remember?'

I squeezed her hand.

'I was holding your hand and you were close beside me. I remember feeling that I never wanted to let you go. People went about so, doing their business, but the accident had made everyone a mother, made everyone a father, regardless of whether they had lost a child or no.'

Mother's lips were red and dry. She let out a long breath. Her hand was wrapped around mine. We were walking there again.

'We passed her. You were beside me. She moaned as we passed her, a pile of rags there, barely alive. But then from behind us she called out – a horrible cry.'

One child dead and one child living;
All children dead and no forgiving

'And when I heard the words I knew.'

I remembered. The woman had been some kind of witch, or monster that had found its way into town from the moors.

'I knew,' mother repeated.

'Knew what?' I asked.

But I knew.

'That Tom would die,' mother said.

I closed my eyes.

'That,' mother said, 'was the curse upon our family. For all that we did, and for all that we knew. It could not have been otherwise.'

Tom had only just been born.

'You were just a little girl, not yet six years old, but already you understood these things. My poor little wonderful Lucy, so sharp, so . . . grown-up. You insisted on caring for him as if he were one of your own. Your father gone, and I unable to live as I had before. John was about to set off for school. And so it was you, Lucy.'

I felt the hand again.

'You were the one.'

'Those were the circumstances, mother,' I said.

'For eight years,' she went on, 'we wondered – you wondered – what would become of him. Mary Toole, she tried her best too, but—'

I could not help but start at the name.

'Why are you thinking of that dreadful woman?'

'I know, Lucy. I always knew from the start. You wanted her—'

Gone, I wanted to say. *I wanted the woman gone*. But I was not about to say anything of the kind, for it would only lead to something that would further disturb us both.

'When she fell on the back stairs,' mother said, 'you did not call out for anyone. Mr Jayne found you there on the landing, staring down at her. You were—'

'It was a shock, mother,' I said.

'I know, my child,' mother said. 'My sweet child, who carried so much. It was not your fault. She slipped – the woman slipped. But in an awful way, I do understand that you counted it as a blessing that she—'

'Mother, must we?' I said. 'At a time like this?'

But mother insisted.

'She was not what was trying to take Tom.'

'Oh mother!' I let out.

She had always blamed me for it. She was talking of Mary Toole and the whole wretched thing when she should have been trying to rest. These memories had somehow given her strength, though they should have been the very things that weakened her.

'I can never pretend to have seen the things he saw. But I know what he saw. *I know*, Lucy – and you do too. You know, my daughter. Perhaps you've seen, or have only wanted to see. But whatever the case, you know.'

'I do know, mother.'

'And now John. Now the horrible things have come for John too. He has the same look in his eyes, all the time now. The same look as our little Tom. And I will tell you something, Lucy – something I have rarely dared think about, and have never dared to utter.'

She paused. Her hand was still wrapped around mine.

'There was a time when your father had that look, too.'

'Father?' I said.

'Yes,' mother said. 'Your father saw them.'

Then she pulled her hand away from mine, and clutched the sheet.

'Of course he would never say so, to himself or anyone else. But he did.'

Father. Tom. John. The terrible line. She was confirming something I had always felt, but had never truly known.

'He knew, Lucy,' mother went on. 'He knew what was going to happen.'

'That what was going to happen?' I gasped.

She closed her eyes, trembled, shook her head. She was seeing it all over again, as if the souls from that day were parading before her.

'He knew,' she said. 'And he sent them in anyway.'

I looked at her.

'What?' I said.

'There was so much more to it,' she continued, 'so much that no one ever knew. Mr Luckhurst, the devil take him, made sure of it. There was a man, to whom it was said that your father had often advanced wages. I cannot remember the name – Ferris or some such. But your father did this for many. It endeared the workers to him. The man's two children were often sick. Your father was kind to him, or at least it seemed so. But the man's wife . . . It was the man's wife, whom your father—'

'Mother,' I whispered.

'They lived in Morwellham, not far from the quay. Many of our workers did. It was remote enough from the town, from the operations. Your father was always careful.'

He was careful, our father. We all knew how much we needed to be.

'This couple, they were one of the families who had lost one of their children. The father had come out unscathed, and one of his boys had been amongst the few who had survived. But the other boy that was with them that day – he was lost. Afterwards, your father went to the house, apparently to console the mother. Some said that he had been visiting her there for years. The husband came home. He surmised things, but he did not act. He nursed his rage quietly, until—'

'How . . .' I said, 'how do you know these things?'

'Mr Luckhurst,' mother replied. 'Mr Luckhurst knew it all.'

She was talking at such a pace, and the rasp in her voice was worsening. But I can say with confidence that she herself appeared almost – comfortable.

'Lucy,' she said. 'It was no accident.'

I stiffened.

'When they saw your father at the bottom of the lime kiln, all assumed that he had stumbled and fallen. But when they got down to him, and finally turned him over, they found that his face had been gashed.'

My breath stopped.

'And next to him was the billhook used to do it. Someone wanted us to know. Someone wanted everyone to know.'

I should have choked. I should have collapsed. Or at the very least I should have done something – anything – to stop the flow of mother's hideous words. But I did nothing. I could do nothing. All of it was believable.

'You will want to know how such a ghastly thing was kept quiet,' mother said.

I breathed out, but did not move.

'That was Mr Luckhurst,' mother said. 'That was his magic.'

'People talk,' I said.

'They do,' mother affirmed. 'The villagers all talked, but in the end it was nothing.'

I had heard all of her words, but again the words did not move me. I was overcome with stillness – the only thing that could absorb so much confusion and shame. What had happened to them then, this family that in the end had fallen into ruin? Had the father been tried and convicted – sent abroad? Had the mother and the other child gone away?

And then, of course, there was the child I had seen that day out on the moors – the little blackened creature with the terrified and brilliant eyes. His face came back to me now. That wretched, terrified face. I had seen him, and he had seen me. He could have been one – or all of them.

'In the house in Devon,' mother said, 'you will find the billhook. In the top drawer of the linen press, if it is still there.'

Another long breath escaped her.

'If anything is still there,' she said.

It was wretched. Everything that mother was saying was wretched. But the only shock I could honestly claim was that none of it was shocking at all. In the end, I suppose, the unfolding of my entire life had prepared me for nothing less than such moments. And what would have burned hot in so many others, instead burned within me as a single question.

'Does John know?' I said.

Mother shook her head.

'I never told him,' she said. 'It would have broken him beyond repair.'

Her head tilted.

'Ah!' she exclaimed suddenly, her eyes widening.

I turned and looked behind me to see if anyone had entered the room. There was no one there, and the door was closed, framed by the birds that swirled within the paper. I turned back towards mother. She was looking beyond me now, not so much at the wall, but at something perhaps in between. And whatever it was, it communicated both pleasure and pain, for mother's face, in this sudden trance, was neither anguished nor enraptured, but rather both of those things at once. She cooed softly, then smiled, then frowned and smiled again. None of the emotion that travelled across her face came or went with any sense of consistency.

'Mother,' I said, 'what is it?'

She reached out her hand.

'Ah!' she sighed again.

There was much more of a rasp to the sigh this time. But she said no more in the darkness of that terrible night, and soon, like a child, she had fallen into a peaceful sleep. I sat with her there, watching her breath go in and out, that soft rasp lessening and lessening until at last her breathing was quiet. I fell asleep in the chair next to her, and the room grew cold, and nothing else visited save for the first strands of dawn. I slept there for a long time, until those strands had grown bright, and the sunlight piercing into the cold air of the room told me that the usual hour for rising had passed. I stood up to move the curtains – it was already one of those brilliant cold days. But when the sun streamed in and shone upon my mother, it shone upon her – dead.

XVII

THE STAPLETON-GRACES, for all their obsequiousness, were extremely helpful during those days following mother's death. They were of course already connected with Mr Murray, the undertaker, who arrived with Mr Stapleton-Grace to collect mother; and they knew, in that old guard sort of way how to get things done, and how to begin and end every sort of matter with the least amount of fuss.

But, this being a family matter, and all family matters being about the company, Mr Rivers was necessarily involved. I had no choice but to involve him because attempting to exclude him in any way would have been looked upon with suspicion. Mother was to be buried up in Highgate with her own parents, and Mr Rivers, knowing the custodian there, worked with Mr Stapleton-Grace to do what needed to be done. In the end, there wound up being very little for me to worry about, because Mr Rivers had arranged everything so elegantly. It was miraculous, the way Mr Rivers could propel things forward. The whole world seemed to want to do his bidding, and quickly.

There were notices, and kind ones, about mother and the company – about how she had met father at the start of Mr Peel's second government, and how her father and that gentleman had worked together on various reforms.

Of course, father had been no great admirer of Mr Peel, and had made many public denouncements against him, but none of that was mentioned, and all of the notices that appeared had only the most genial words to say about mother. One never would have thought that these celebratory remembrances could come from the very same periodicals that had published such sensational reports about 'walls of death'. In mother's notices at least, any association with these scandals had, perhaps out of some kind of temporary respect, retreated.

There were many at the service, though not as many as there could have been, thanks to the careful arrangements of Mr Rivers and Mr Stapleton-Grace. I did not want people, nor did John – poor John who could not even walk, and who was forced to put on such a show on such a hideous day. He was in a wheel-chair for the coming and going, my brother, pushed by our ever-faithful Mr Jayne, who struggled as he manoeuvred him. At one point I had suggested replacing Mr Jayne with Susan, or even myself, but Mr Rivers insisted on keeping all lines in order, and said that it would not have looked right.

My dear John – how I can still see you on that damp, late November day, no sun shining, no light on your face, your shoulders slumped, your coughs frequent, your body doing its best to stay upright. You were trying, my brother, I knew you were, because even as a boy you understood your sense of duty, and as a man you had become no less dutiful. You needed to do what you did that day for us, and for the company. But how terrible it must have been when the chair was lifted and carried over the uneven terrain . . . when those other faithful men from the company,

191

Mr Ismay amongst them, took you into their charge so that you could be with me at the grave, by my side until the end. Know this: I had tried to spare you this horrible indignation. I would have understood. Mother would have understood. The world – the company – would have understood. But Mr Rivers had insisted, and I could not fight him.

I hope you can forgive me.

You see, my plan was forming, and though I had no sense of its ending, I at least knew that if I didn't manage to fix upon something soon, my brother would die. Yes – that is what was happening: my brother was dying. Dying at the hands of the infernal beast that preyed upon him. John had always struggled, had never been completely well. But now everything about his condition was permanently down, and never up. And it was all because of the deathly presence that we had, of our own volition, let into our house.

I needed to get him out.

But then I did something you will think quite strange. After the funeral, I sent both of them back in. Yes, I know, given the state of anxiety I have just described, it is impossible to think that I would have sent my brother back to the house with Mr Rivers, without me. But I did it. Because, you see, Mr Rivers still needed my brother in order to continue with his own plan – until he married me, that is. With mother now gone there was every reason to believe that Mr Rivers would lean even more heavily on John to press forward with his dreadful plan of making himself one of us. And so in the most bizarre way, contrary to everything I have said so far, I felt that John, for the moment, would not be harmed in his company.

Perhaps I was wrong, though, for the threats were ever present.

'You should not be out walking alone,' Mr Rivers said to me. 'Not on a day like this.'

'There have been worse days, Mr Rivers,' I said. 'And Susan will be with me.'

'Neither of you should be out alone,' he persisted.

'Are we children?' I said curtly.

We were standing at the carriages, all lined up to take us home. And Mr Jayne was working with another man to put John inside.

'Very well,' he said. 'I shall see your brother back into bed.'

'Where he should have been all the while,' I said.

'Jayne, take care now!' Mr Rivers blurted out suddenly.

Then I turned and left the wretch.

Susan and I walked through the corridors of mossy tombs, and once we were out of sight of the main thoroughfare I dismissed her. Of course she protested, saying that she did not want to leave me, but I assured her that I would be fine, and that she would best serve me by taking herself off to the market to purchase sundries for Mrs Dawes. She left, and I was at last alone with my thoughts which, even before mother's death, had become so tangled with what my next steps should be. The truth is, I was trapped with no way of breaking out. Mr Rivers had already established such a firm hold on everything.

And then there were his plans. His hideous plans to drench our world in his poison. I wondered if John knew, or had ever surmised. John – did you ever, even for a moment, consider the idea that the thing you loved so much might be the same thing that was trying to kill you?

I walked. The hills rolled down towards the city, spotted by fields and trees until they met the white edge of the metropolis. All was grey on that wet grey day, and the mist moved through the graves like so many channels of a river. Mother was dead and I was the only one left, not that mother had been doing very much to protect us of late. She had, as I have written, become something of a child herself, even more in need of the same kind of unquestioning devotion that I had been carrying out all my life. But still, to have her there, the only one who might understand things . . . it provided some solace, even if those things were never or rarely talked about.

And now she was gone – gone! And I was utterly alone. Oh mother – with all that you knew, how could you destroy yourself, and leave us?

And then there was father. What I had learned about him – the horror of it. Slashed with a billhook and thrown to the bottom of one of our own kilns. The rage that had done that – the disturbing justice of it. What frightened me most was not that I was not shocked by it, but that I could intimately understand how such a thing could happen.

Yes, dear father. There are bogs. There are dangers.

I continued walking along the uneven paths and came across the carcass of a large rat. Or perhaps it was a weasel – I couldn't tell, it was so decomposed. It must have been rotting there for a very long time, and would continue there, rotting, until the rain finally washed the last bits of it away, or someone else came along and swept what was left of it from the path.

I walked further, and eventually I arrived at an enormous tomb – a hideous, colossal thing made of Portland stone, rising up from the graves around it like the most arrogant of cathedrals. It had a pyramid-shaped roof, huge bronze doors decorated with animals, and ostentatious rows of columns carved into panels around the walls. What husband or father would have made such a desperate thing, visible from miles all around? Who was inside of it? What did they look like now? Could there possibly have been anything left of them?

'Extraordinary,' the soft voice said behind me. 'But what does any of it matter, in the end?'

I turned.

'Mr Ismay!'

'I'm sorry, Miss Braithwhite, I did not mean to startle you.'

He noticed me looking behind him.

'I am alone,' he said. 'They are all gone.'

He stepped forward.

'But I must be quick, and we must be very careful. Come, please, out of the main way.'

He motioned for us to move off the path, and guided me around the side of the great tomb.

'Miss Braithwhite,' he whispered, 'it is very unsafe for me to be here.'

I was surprised not by the idea, but that he too seemed to understand it so well.

'Then you know,' I said. 'It has become more than suspicion for you?'

He nodded.

'It is very unsafe,' he repeated, his lip slightly trembling. 'I've put both of us in great danger by following you.'

I was sure that it was true.

'Tell me, Mr Ismay. You need not spare your words.'

'I have wanted to write to you,' he began, 'but even that I was afraid to do. So I have been thinking instead of how I could somehow reach you, when this unfortunate turning . . .'

He bowed his head and I offered my hand.

'I am so deeply sorry, Miss Braithwhite . . . for everything.'

There was so much emotion in even these few words. He trembled. Mr Ismay had loved mother, too.

'Tell me, Mr Ismay,' I said.

He released my hand, and gathered himself. Then he moved us even closer to the side of the vault.

'Of my own interests I cannot be concerned,' he said. 'But you and Mr Braithwhite, whom I have served since the days of your father . . . I cannot . . . Your . . .'

'Please, Mr Ismay.'

'I feel your brother's very life may be at stake.'

'I know,' I said.

'You know?'

'I do, most certainly. But tell me what it is that you mean.'

'The accounts, miss. They—'

And I realised in that moment that Mr Ismay was unsteady. Something had happened – something had shaken him. I had never known him without his resolve.

'The accounts are deficient,' he said. 'Not dramatically, but I have been noticing, for some time—'

'What do you mean, deficient?' I said.

'The numbers,' he said hesitatingly. 'Well . . . things are missing.'

'Missing?' I said. 'You mean someone is—'

'Stealing – yes,' he replied. 'And the troubling thing is the signatures. The signatures on the accounts are—'

'Ah!' I exclaimed. 'They are *his* then?'

Mr Ismay nodded gravely.

'Most decidedly, they are his,' he said.

'Well then, he must be confronted.'

'It is not within my power to do that,' Mr Ismay said.

'What of the numbers, though? Do you have proof?'

'Not exactly,' Mr Ismay said, 'because, well, the thing seems to be . . . it's being done ever so carefully. Only those with the keenest eyes at the company might notice. Until, of course, it is too late.'

'This is treacherous, Mr Ismay,' I said. 'If Mr Rivers is guilty, we must find a way to expose him.'

Mr Ismay's face sank.

'Ah, no, miss,' he said. 'I'm afraid I've not been clear.'

'What do you mean?'

Mr Ismay looked down, then up at me again.

'The signatures on the accounts are not those of Mr Rivers.'

'Please, Mr Ismay,' I said. 'I need you to be very plain with me.'

He looked away this time, but there was no comfort in the distance.

'The signatures . . .' he stumbled, 'are your brother's.'

My heart stopped.

'Mr Ismay,' I managed. 'Are you saying that my brother—'

'I am saying nothing of the kind, miss.'

'Are they forgeries then?'

'Perhaps. Or in fact his signature, under some . . . influence.'

He paused. There was such a look of fear in his eyes. And sorrow – deep sadness at what he was having to tell me. I had never imagined that Mr Rivers's treachery could have grown so much worse; but here before me was evidence that the infection was even more terrible.

I waited a moment.

'And what do you suggest?' I finally asked.

'Have your brother cease all interaction immediately,' he said. 'At least until I can devise a means to best reconcile the books.'

'I'm afraid that will be very difficult,' I said. 'The company is the one thing that keeps him going.'

'You must!' Mr Ismay exclaimed. 'Somehow, some way, you must—'

'Mr Rivers is ever present,' I emphasised. 'He will see. He will encourage him.'

'I know,' Mr Ismay said. 'But you must do whatever you can to try. If what is happening is permitted to continue, then, well, the consequences—'

'I know, Mr Ismay,' I said. 'None of us are safe.'

A horrible thing, a horrible thought – that one could no longer find safety in one's own home. How had this all happened? How had I failed so exquisitely? I had spent my whole life trying to stop it, and yet here it all was, pouring in.

But the thoughts were beginning to come to me, and everything was not lost. The demon had his weaknesses. It was up to me now to exploit them.

I pondered.

'Mr Ismay,' I said at last, 'if Mr Rivers were to need to go to the Continent, or even America, who would run the company, in his absence?'

Mr Ismay curled his lip.

'It is doubtful that he would ever go anywhere for so long as to require that.'

'I know,' I said, 'but supposing—'

'Well, there is of course Mr Muggs in the Tavistock office, a very capable fellow. And there is myself here in London, along with Mr Adams. Between us we would manage. Why do you ask?'

'After the horrible loss of Mr Luckhurst,' I said, 'you can imagine how concerned I've been – how concerned we've been – that so much of the company's fortune depends on one person.'

Mr Ismay nodded.

'Well, it does and it doesn't,' he said. 'Like so many things.'

He had lightened somewhat since he had first approached me, though he did look around once more as he prepared to leave.

'I'm sorry to have come upon you on such a day with such information,' he said. 'But there is so much at stake, and we must do everything we can to—'

I stopped him.

'I am so grateful to you, Mr Ismay. Beyond what any of us could describe.'

He took my hand and he squeezed it, and his eyes shone with the beginnings of tears. Good and loyal Mr Ismay, whose intentions had always been pure. He stepped back out into the path and in a moment he was gone, and there I stood alone in the cemetery, accompanied only by a crowd of questions. Out of all of them, though, there was one that repeatedly surfaced to the top: did Mr Rivers want to take the company, or simply ruin it? And, well . . . I could have asked the very same question with regard to John. For in taking my brother, Mr Rivers would also ruin him. Our family would be cast into infamy – all according to his plan. And then, there was the other question, the elusive answer to which was the one thing impelling me forward: how was I going to stop him, and save my brother and the company all at once?

I stepped back into the path, where only a moment ago Mr Ismay had been, when I heard a rustling in a bush not far from where we had been standing. A branch moved, a leaf fell, and a shape made itself visible through the broken foliage. Then, like a frightened animal, the shape crouched for a moment, and ran.

'Rob!' I called out.

But the boy had already fled.

XVIII

AN UNEVENTFUL WEEK passed by after mother's funeral, though my mind continued to dwell morosely on that day. Then, in those first cold days of December, Mr Jayne died too. Mrs Dawes found him lying peacefully in his bed one morning, after he had failed to come out for breakfast. A few days earlier he had twisted his ankle on the back stair-case, even after all those years of negotiating those awful steps without error. And so, even though that small injury could not have been the cause of his death, I could not help but think that perhaps, somehow, it was the very thing that had led to his demise.

Mr Jayne's funeral service was private, in a small church-yard in Twickenham, where his family had originally come from, and where a few distant cousins still remained. We said goodbye to him on a day that lashed with rain. I thought it best to keep John at home so my brother did not attend.

Our house was growing quieter. Just John and me and Susan now, and Mrs Dawes down below. There was no point in looking for a replacement for Mr Jayne, as John's needs ran beyond what any footman in London could possibly deliver. Taking care of him was a task that needed to be carried out, day and night, by me. Mr Rivers was also of the opinion that we should not be bringing another person into our house; but that had everything to do with his effort to isolate me, and nothing to do with any kind of belief in my strength.

John thanked me. Through his sunken eyes and pale skin and persistent coughs he thanked me. He felt so badly, my brother, still wanting to shield me from the trials and eruptions that had always plagued us. But he could not. He loved me – that was something I never doubted – but what he saw, what haunted him from the walls, had now become his constant company. I wished that I could have shared his burden, but it was not something I was able to do. For me, the dark colours and twisted patterns on our walls revealed nothing more than what was right there before me.

I meandered – there is no other word to describe it. Night would close in and, with John sound asleep, I would ramble through our handsome house, from room to beautiful room. I walked as if in a dream, listening with no sound coming, and I wondered, wandering, why I had so often looked but had never been able to see. What was it about those shapes, those malevolent patterns that rolled out before me, that had blinded me from perceiving what all of this would inevitably come to? We had been so happy – or at least we thought we were – and I had never wanted any other picture. Yes, as a girl I had longed for the west country, but I could create fields and hills here just the same. And I did – that is until the patterns changed and our entire world began to unfurl. There I am, clear-headed as any day, remembering Tom, remembering mother, remembering poor Mr Jayne. And yet a mist forms in my eyes and I cannot see the things I think I can see. A mist forms and I cannot see the shape of my little brother. Nor the shape of my mother, and all the others – so many others – shining before me like angels.

We went on, and I did not know how long the uncertainty would last. With John so weakened and mother now gone, there was nothing preventing Mr Rivers from carrying out the most devious parts of his campaign. I could construct various scenarios, but there was no way for me to know for sure how or when he planned to move, or what his final act of treachery would be. I stared at the walls with no choice but to wait – the vines in the patterns now strangling themselves, it seemed, with the intimate knowledge of my own frustration. How I wanted to tear them down, to make them the weapons of my own defence. But I did not, and instead merely counted the hours and days with extreme patience.

That is, until the day finally came when everything changed before me.

Mr Rivers was there, working with John in his room, though what particular work my brother could even do at that point was a mystery to me. Mr Rivers, in all this time, had been insistent on not changing the pattern – on continuing his visits as consistently as possible so as to prevent John from 'dulling'. In theory, and under any other circumstances, I would have thought such an approach wise, but of course the effect that Mr Rivers was having upon my brother distressed me more and more with every encounter. The devil knew this, he could see his own effect on me plainly, and to taunt me he would on occasion invite me in as their business was winding down. At which point John would inevitably launch into a grand soliloquy about how Mr Rivers was guaranteeing our longevity for the next one hundred years.

But on that day when it turned, Mr Rivers was there, and something happened to confirm that he was not the all-powerful thing I had believed him to be. He was, as I said, working with John in his room, and I was waiting nearby in the drawing room, as I always did during those visits. At one point I looked out of one of the side windows and saw movement near the back gate, and so I went all the way down to the kitchen, and then proceeded out the back door.

I crossed the garden and threw open the gate, and this time Rob was there, but did not run.

'And why are you back around here then, Rob?' I said.

'He told me, miss,' Rob said, sheepishly. 'He told me to stay out of sight today.'

'And why is that?' I asked.

But Rob did not answer.

'Miss,' he said, hurriedly, 'you must go back in. He will see you!'

'And so what if he does?' I said. 'This is my house.'

'Oh, miss . . .' Rob stammered.

'Now stop this nonsense, boy,' I said, 'and tell me – have you been enjoying the sweet cakes I've been leaving you?'

Rob stopped his fidgeting.

'Oh, very much, miss,' he said. 'They are a treat for a cove. Like nothing a cove should have.'

'And why not?' I said. 'You should have them. Lord knows your master will not indulge you.'

'No, miss,' he said.

'And so he knows that you were here, then, the last time? That I fed you?'

'Yes, miss.'

'You told him?'

'No, miss.'

'Then how did he know?'

'He knew.'

'How?'

'He just knows.'

'Very well,' I grimaced, 'but he shall not know of today, and he shall not know of what I've been leaving you, because we've both been very careful – isn't that right, Rob?'

Rob nodded.

'And I know that you are doing your duty to watch over me and protect me, as a fine boy of even your years is able to do.'

He looked at the ground. He was a fine young man, too good to be in such perfidious care.

'Now, Rob,' I said, 'I am going to go back inside, but before I do, I want you to see something.'

The boy stood there, and I stepped fully out of the gate and into the walkway. Then I turned and stared straight up at my brother's window.

'Do you see that?' I said.

I did not avert my gaze, but simply faced the window for some moments. No one came.

Rob also looked up.

'What, miss?' he said.

'Do you see that?' I repeated. 'What do you see?'

'Nothing, miss.'

'Precisely. You see nothing, Rob. And that is exactly what you have to fear – nothing.'

I touched his face. It was clean and smooth – unlike the last time.

'Now,' I said, 'I am going to go back inside, and we shall talk again sometime. You know that's true, don't you?'

'Yes, miss,' the boy replied.

'And you know that, whatever might happen between you and your master, you can find safety here, at this gateway and in this house, because you know who I am – isn't that right, Rob?'

'Yes, miss.'

'Who am I?'

'Miss Braithwhite.'

'And what is this house?'

'The house of Braithwhite & Company.'

'That's right. And though you are too poor and unfortunate to understand this, you must believe me when I tell you that there is nothing the company cannot do.'

The boy of course would never smile, but his mouth did something that was like a smile, which told me that I had reached him. I left him there and went inside, and made my way back through the kitchen as if nothing had occurred. Upstairs, in the hall, I could still hear the echoes of Mr Rivers's voice, sometimes followed by the faintest responses from John, but more often followed by silence. I returned to the drawing room. I paced and read and waited. And at last John's door opened and the creature stepped out. I stood in place waiting for him, like a sentinel by my own window, and this time Mr Rivers did not rush past the door. Instead, he paused at the threshold and studied me, looking upon me as a mortal looks upon an angel.

'Miss Braithwhite,' he said, smiling.

There was a breathlessness in his eyes. But his true intentions could not be concealed by anything he might have done.

I nodded. I smiled. I invited him to sit down.

'Tell me, Mr Rivers,' I said. 'How do you find my brother?'

He hesitated, looking at me, and then said something or other about John's delight with the returns. It was clear he had no knowledge of what I had just done with Rob downstairs. I watched as the colours of our drawing-room paper swirled, and collected themselves into a violent pattern. And as I saw them move, and detected no power of movement from Mr Rivers, I knew that, for once, I had outfoxed him.

It was twilight by the time Mr Rivers left that day, and my brother did not emerge from his room for the rest of the evening. At the dinner hour, I tried to take John some tea and toast on a tray, but the door was locked, and when I called to him he said that he was fine and asked to be left alone. I needed to use my best judgement in these instances, for my duty was to walk that finest of lines between attending to John fully and allowing him his privacy. The voice that reached me through the door that evening had been clear and calm – so calm that it made me long to see him, to confirm with my own eyes that he was settled. But in that moment I retreated and did as John requested, and returned myself to the drawing room to read until the sun went down.

I fell asleep to Mr Wordsworth – *There was a time when meadow, grove, and stream* – and the hour was not late when I reawakened. I think Susan must have been there while I dozed because the lamps were half lit and the room was very tidy. I could hear her now downstairs scraping at the coal grate in one of the fireplaces – a regular, abrasive sound that was not loud, but that travelled through the halls nonetheless.

I went to John's door and knocked. There was no response. I whispered his name through the door, but still there was no sound.

I listened. More silence – no signs of movement or breath.

The door was locked. I unlocked it and pushed it forward as carefully as I could. Then the chill hit me all at once, and the cold air rushed by me. I opened the door further – John's window was open! And there, like a feeble fawn curled up in its little den was my brother, covers wrapped around him, sleeping as peacefully as a child.

I rushed over to the window and closed it. The sound did not wake John. I added coals to the fire and stirred them. The room was a room of ice.

I set my candle down on the mantel and looked about the room. It had been tidied, though by whom I could not determine. The papers on the table were still far from organised, but the great mounds spilling over each other were now ordered and clustered into much neater heaps. The accumulation of papers over these past few months had been considerable, and what a miracle it had been, not to mention impressive, that John, even in his condition, had somehow been managing to keep track of so much in his head. Perhaps he himself deeply felt what I had surmised but never said: that the company was the very thing that was keeping him going.

John breathed out – the softest and gentlest breath – and I went over to the bed and sat beside him. I hope you will forgive my noting the most obvious of associations, but what I saw in that moment was – Tom. In his slumber John had given up the struggle against everything that haunted him, and had returned for a short time to the quiescence of his childhood. His face was soft, his eyes at rest, his skin smooth and beautiful even though it lacked colour. He was in the state that I yearned for him to be in always – asleep without nightmares, dreaming of hills and streams, the colours of a brooding landscape offering him his happiness and his freedom.

I returned to the drawing room, turned up the lamp, and collected my book. But before sitting, I made a round and looked out of all the windows. The lamps had been lit and the street was aglow. There was no one outside in the dry and darkening cold.

I read. Then I slept. Then I awoke and slept again. The fire in the drawing room warmed me, and despite everything that was happening I felt safe and cocooned. I dozed, and at one point I heard a cry in my mind – mother. That last cry on that last night. Oh mother – why did you abandon me?

Then, at some point – I cannot say when – an ember in the fire exploded. It shot out and I awakened.

And then I heard John scream.

For yes, the sound this time was unmistakable – not one of the dreamlike, shapeless sounds that had so disturbed me in the past. John's voice cried out – one chilling, horrible scream, as if there, not far from me, a dagger of ice had stabbed straight into his heart.

I rushed in – the room was frozen – and John was on the floor, clutching every part of the bedclothes around him. Again, the window was open and the invading air was like death. I collapsed next to John. He was shivering. He was crying. And from the window, the great flow of cold air streamed in, and John stared there, as if the air itself possessed some kind of form.

'John,' I said deliberately, though I had begun to shiver with him. 'I am here. It is all right.'

Then I squeezed him and stood up to move towards the window, but as I did so he tore at me violently, like some madman or rabid savage.

'No!' he screamed. 'Let them out! Let them out!'

He was seeing them – they were there. All around him.

'John!' I exclaimed, pulling myself away from him.

But he held onto me, his shivering body spilling out of the tangled sheets.

'John!' I exclaimed again.

I loosened his hands and pushed him away from me. He fell back, a trembling animal, and I got away from him and ran over to slam the window.

The cold air stopped; the room was still.

'Let them out,' John whispered.

Then my brother curled himself up and made an awful sound. I left him there, writhing, for the most important thing was the fire. I stirred the failing coals, added kindling, and poked everything about in the grate. The fire burned and I returned to John, and draped the sheets and the blankets all around him.

He calmed. The room would remain very cold. The coals would take time to grow hot again.

I held onto John. He was a mere child in my arms. And I hated all the ghastliness that had brought us to this.

John shivered.

'What is it?' I said.

Though I knew what it was.

John's head was on my breast. He clutched at the sheets, and at me – at anything that might protect him from the very air around him. The visions had been growing worse, but there was something about this episode that told me that the whole thing had changed. Something horrendous had occurred.

I held John. I stroked his hair.

'What is it?' I said. 'What has happened?'

John breathed. He was gathering himself. And his strength was beginning to come back.

'He was here,' John finally said.

'Who?' I said.

'Rivers.'

'Mr Rivers?'

'Yes, Rivers,' John said. 'He was here, in this room.'

'Yes, he was, John. He was here some hours ago.'

'No, he was here – just now.'

'John—'

'I tell you, Lucy, he was here in this very room. As plain as you are here before me!'

'That's not possible,' I said.

'It does not matter what is possible, and what is not. He was here, and I saw him.'

Then John described how, as he had been turning over in his bed, Mr Rivers had crept in through the open window, like some sort of hideous night creature.

'I don't know how he did it,' John said. 'He crawled in like a spider. At first I thought it was some horrible dream, but then he stood up – stood defiantly before me – and he looked around the whole room, as if searching for things to take.'

'John' I said. 'This is not possible. This is fancy.'

But with Mr Rivers, as I have said before, there was nothing that was not possible.

Then John pushed himself away from me.

'Lucy!' he cried. 'You must listen!'

Then John proceeded to tell me how Mr Rivers, standing at the foot of his bed, had said the most awful things to him. How our manager, in the most nonchalant way imaginable, had soliloquised about how we – all of us – were hated. 'There is not a man employed at the company,' he said, 'who wouldn't be glad at heart to see this family ruined. Who does not hate you, secretly. Who does not wish you evil. And who would not turn upon you, if they had the power.'

Then, John said, Mr Rivers began pacing about the room, tall and malevolent, like a spectre. John protested, but one look from Mr Rivers silenced him, and my brother pulled the sheets around him, as if in them he could find protection.

'So proud,' Mr Rivers said. 'So . . . *worthy*.'

And he smiled a ghastly smile, as my brother crouched in fear.

'Imagine,' the treacherous demon went on, 'just imagine, for one moment that your brother hadn't died in the comfort of his own bed, but had instead taken his last breaths in the darkness of a mine. That your father hadn't met his end in a way that no one talked about, but had rather been transported for life, ignominiously, for a crime he had been driven to by madness. That your mother hadn't lived out the rest of her luxurious existence in this house, but had instead grown miserable and so absent-minded that the streets became the only place for her. And imagine, just imagine, Mr Braithwhite, if you had been the child of that woman, a strong and healthy and determined child, and had defied everything and everyone to work your way up through the company that you believed it was your destiny to rule. Imagine how if all of that had been true, Mr Braithwhite, how different life would have been for us all!'

The horror of what he was saying was too much, and my brother listened, helpless, unable to move or protest. He was a prisoner of our manager – the man who had come to claim his revenge. The shadow of Mr Rivers's wickedness had at last become very real.

His smile, John said, was the worst thing of all. I could see it glimmering too. The great white teeth wanting to bite.

Then, with the kindness of an uncle or a friend, Mr Rivers sat down next to John on the bed.

'He told me other things,' John said. 'Things that I had never thought I could believe. I did not want to hear any of it, but he forced me to listen.'

They were more horrible things – about father, about the company. And as Mr Rivers spoke, John felt the words seeping into him, like venom.

'I was helpless to stop listening,' John said, 'but at last I understood.'

Then John buried his head in his hands.

'This cursed family! This company!'

I hated Mr Rivers. What I heard made me furious and I hated him. The man was poison – poison in the shape of a hideous flower. But sometimes, as horrible as it is to have to think it, the poison is the same thing as the antidote.

'I listened to him,' John said. 'He spoke calmly. He was not angry. And everything he said to me was true. I already knew.'

John stopped for a moment, pressed his hands harder over his eyes.

'I don't think you can possibly understand what he has meant to me.'

My breath stopped in my throat. How much longer would I refuse to see it?

'No, John,' I said. 'I do.'

John went quiet then, and his remaining energy faded. I got him back into his bed, fixed the covers, smoothed his hair. Mr Rivers had fed him, had awakened his hunger. And yet John would never be able to comprehend the immense danger we were all in.

Mr Rivers had closed in on us. And so what was I to do? I, Lucy Braithwhite – the only one who could see things as they were.

My heart pounded with such rage as I stared at the patterns across the walls.

'Show me,' I said to them. 'If there is a time, then it is now!'

The green shapes moved as shadows and there was no light that could possibly brighten them. And all the confusion and fury and disquiet I had ever felt exploded in a burst of colour. My head swooned, my eyes burned, and the walls cried out in agony. And everything I had never been able to see, or hadn't wanted to see, I saw.

My mission, my duty – one horrible charge – suddenly and at last possessed me. And I could do it. I could put an end to the whole thing.

For I too was the company.

XIX

MR RIVERS HAD said, more than once, that people hated us. But what I now understood was that *he* was amongst those who hated us. Given everything I had discovered, everything I now knew to be true, he was perhaps the one person who hated us more than anyone else. He hated me, my brother, our family – the company – all while desperately wanting to be one of us. He would, I was convinced, do whatever he needed to do to destroy us, though whether that might also have meant destroying himself in the process, I did not know. He was full of vengeance, and in his rage he would destroy much more than my family. He would drive the whole company to such a point of destruction that thousands, perhaps hundreds of thousands of others would perish. For that, he had the formulas, and our ever-abundant supplies of arsenic. And with John's blessing, he could sow and harvest all the hateful destruction he had been dreaming of.

I had only one charge, then, and the charge was very clear: I needed to destroy Julian Rivers.

First thing the next morning, I made my way down to the counting house, where I found the long tables of our accountants and clerks consumed in their work. Our men did what they did with extra care and thought – successors to those who had been carrying out the mission of the company for generations. But none of them could fully understand the great conspiracy of which they had all become a part. Like worms in rotting fruit, they were all burrowing through the company, unwittingly eating away at its show of beauty and grace.

Mr Ismay rose from one of the tables as soon as he saw me and approached.

'Miss Braithwhite,' he said, glancing back behind him into the office. 'A pleasure. And—'

'I have come to see Mr Rivers,' I said.

Mr Ismay's expression grew agitated.

'I do not think that is a good idea this morning, Miss Braithwhite.'

I could see Mr Rivers deeper in the office, his slim body hunched over the desk in father's glass chamber.

'And why is that?' I said.

'He came in late,' Mr Ismay said. 'And he is not in good spirits.'

'Not in good spirits?' I said. 'And since when do I need to be concerned with my manager's spirits?'

'Miss Braithwhite . . .' Mr Ismay stammered.

'Excuse me, Mr Ismay.'

I stepped around the man, and walked straight towards father's office.

Mr Rivers did not see me as I drew closer to the glass room upon the dais. He was so deep in whatever was occupying him that, even in that space from which he could survey everything, the closest movement failed to distract him. His brow was furrowed and his eyes looked cold. He was plotting something, no doubt, figuring on how to circumvent this or that obstacle.

There were three small steps that led up to the platform, and as I ascended them, Mr Rivers still did not look up.

I opened the chamber door.

'Yes?' he said, without lifting his head.

'I am sorry to disturb you,' I said.

Then his head shot up. I had done the impossible: I had surprised him. Something like terror stole into his eyes.

But then, as quickly as it had come, the look was gone. He sat up, folded his hands. The eyes darkened.

'How can I help you?' he said flatly.

'May I?' I said, acknowledging the chair in front of the desk.

'Of course,' he said. 'I'm sorry.'

I took my seat, and I was now across from him, face to face. Outside the glass, the office, hive-like, buzzed around us.

'I wanted to thank you,' I said.

'Thank me?' he questioned.

'Yes,' I replied. 'There is much to thank you for. I wanted to thank you – for your visits.'

The corner of his mouth moved, that familiar hint of the dreadful smile.

'I am duty bound,' he said, without smiling.

'You've performed so much more than your duty,' I said.

And he nodded, and leaned forward in the chair.

'But there is more,' he said. 'You didn't come all the way down here just to thank me.'

'Yes.'

He waited. I gathered myself.

'It will come as no surprise to you,' I finally said, 'that my brother has endured yet another unsettling night. And after last night, I could not help but be plunged into all kinds of thoughts.'

He nodded – the hands still folded, the body calm.

'And after last night,' I continued, 'the thought has taken hold of me that the time has come—'

I paused. What I was about to say would change everything. I was accelerating his treacherous plan. But what he would not realise, or at least what I prayed he would not realise, was that in accelerating his plan, I was also advancing my own.

Mr Rivers raised a brow.

'The time has come to move forward,' I said.

I sat and waited. Nothing about him moved. His eyes were fixed, like those of a glaring wolf.

Then, after a moment, he leaned forward again.

'I agree,' he said, rather quietly. 'Mr Braithwhite is in great peril.'

Ah, then – his mind had gone to John! I could not have hoped for anything better.

I waited.

'I think the best thing,' Mr Rivers finally went on, 'would be for your brother to come with me.'

I had of course thought of it – the idea of John going off. That in his mind getting John away from me was a necessary part of it.

'That I cannot condone,' I said. 'My brother will die if he leaves me.'

Then Mr Rivers slapped a furious hand down upon the desk.

'Your brother will die if he *stays*!' he shouted.

Initially that did not make any sense to me, as the words did not fit with anything I had been thinking about him. But then I realised exactly what Mr Rivers was doing. He was trying to equate me with the criminal that *he* was.

'You've grown impatient with me, Mr Rivers,' I said.

'Not so much with you, Miss Braithwhite,' he said, 'as with your dangerous ways and your dangerous remedies.'

'You think me dangerous?'

'I do.'

'And how would you have been any better, Mr Rivers?'

'For one,' he said, 'I would have given your brother what he needed.'

The insolence and – yes – the stupidity. It enraged me. What did this boy from the country understand of the days and nights and years my family had spent in that house?

I hated him.

'You, Miss Braithwhite,' the villain went on, 'you yourself have had daydreams and nightmares that—'

'If I've had nightmares, Mr Rivers,' I interrupted, 'they've been about one thing, and we both know what that is.'

'But do you?' he snapped back at me. 'Do *you* understand what your worst nightmare is?'

He was wretched.

'How dare you speak to me in this manner?'

'I speak plainly,' he said, 'just as I have spoken to your brother.'

His eyes were locked upon me, and I was caught in his merciless vice. And yet, I did not struggle. Turn the vice as you may, Mr Rivers – I will never struggle against you again.

Then he turned it:

'Do you have any idea of what has gone on in that room?'

I was still. He wanted me to flush.

Then he turned it again:

'Do you understand?'

I met him.

'I understand perfectly, Mr Rivers,' I said. 'The *business* that my brother has so unfortunately conducted – conducted I dare suggest under your influence – would mean his total ruination. A fall from which he would never recover.'

Mr Rivers grinned.

'My influence is irrelevant,' he said. 'Your brother has been quite careless with himself. If brought to light, your entire family would never recover.'

My family. Father and mother, and grandfather, and Tom, and every Braithwhite who had ever been a spoke in this dreadful wheel. I could see them – all of them – glaring in at me from the walls. Only, the walls in father's office were glass – the glass that laid bare the company.

'Your brother—' Mr Rivers began.

But I stopped him.

'My brother,' I said, 'is my only concern, and you are right. I will not fight you any longer. Give me a few days' time and we will move forward. I assure you I can be ready.'

He raised the horrible brow again.

'Ah, then,' he said. 'Most excellent.'

'A few days' time,' I repeated, 'and then you and I shall tell him together.'

He smiled.

'That sounds like a fine idea, Miss Braithwhite. I am glad to see that you've finally come around. I am your only answer here. I only wish that you had seen that all along.'

I would not be telling the truth if I said that I was not frightened, for now the thing had been said out loud, and there was no choice but to go through with it.

I looked through the glass.

'I want him to get better,' I whispered. 'It is the only thing I want – for John to get better.'

And then I heard the most horrible laugh – like the shattering of the glass into a thousand pieces.

Mr Rivers had thrown back his head.

'That's precious!' he exclaimed. 'You don't want your brother to get better. Indeed, you never did.'

What a cruel and evil man – a man who understood everything and nothing. How I had allowed such a man to have such power over me at all is a thing that brings me great shame. It is not the shame in *his* mind – the shame that purportedly lurked in my worst nightmares – but rather the shame of simply being a stupid and blind fool. I should have seen everything, everything he was doing from the start. I was foolish to have doubted his real motives for even a second.

But no more.

'Only one question remains, then,' Mr Rivers said.

'Yes.'

'And of course you know what it is.'

'I do.'

Then Mr Rivers reached his hand across my father's desk. His arm rested upon the surface and the elegant fingers uncurled.

'Will you marry me, Miss Braithwhite?'

I took the hand and thought a moment, though I did not need to think. That hand had first touched me months ago – so beautiful, so comforting – in the hour of my greatest need. Little did I notice then what I suddenly noticed now: that the hand contained awful, half-hidden patterns – patterns of work, and of drudgery. Mr Rivers could never have had a hand like my brother's, or mine, for his life could never have been the same. Like the occasional slips in his mellifluous voice, his hands could not conceal where he had come from.

But too much had happened, and none of that mattered. It was all coming to an end now, and this plan would put the end to it.

I looked at the hand, and then into the wicked eyes.

And at last I said:

'I will.'

XX

THERE WERE BOGS. There were dangers.

And there was never a time when I was not afraid to lose John. Even when Tom was still alive, and John was without complaint, I feared that something could at any moment come and take him. Because, you see, as robust as John was, and as fast as he could leap from dry spot to dry spot in the mud, the sense was deep within me that one careless turn or one false step would plunge him into that quivering mire. The bogs held secrets, and bodies, and souls, and while on top the soft undulations stretched out, serenely, for yards, underneath were so many desperate, malignant hands, waiting to tug you down. We were never safe from them. No one was safe. The clutch of the land was grim and purposeful. And though there, out on the moors, we could run and we were free, the threat was always present that something could catch you and not let go.

We had been caught – I had been caught – in the infernal grasp that belonged to Mr Rivers. That grasp had been like a poison so subtle that one had to sicken from it to fully appreciate its power. John was sick. The house was sick. The company was sick. And now, at last, I was sick – sick with understanding of what this whole vile thing meant, and what my duty really should have been from the start. There was one thing, and one thing only, that could now save my brother, and that thing involved the most elaborate and, yes, most terrifying of measures. There was no doubt in my mind that I could do what I needed to do, but one fear continued to haunt me, hour after hour. I would prepare everything, and leave no seam unstitched, but would Mr Rivers, in his infinite treachery, somehow discover my plans before I could finish?

He could not. I would need to make sure of it.

I had but a few days, and of course I would be watched. Outside, Rob sauntered — he did not hide as much any more. The boy walked back and forth across the street between the lamp posts, or hovered on the walkway, close to the wall, near the back gate. We had no secrets. We had an understanding. And on that first day, when I went out of the front door and, from some distance, called out to ask if he would like to accompany me to Covent Garden, he looked about, more embarrassed than astonished, and shook his head. I walked. He trailed behind.

I bought as many groceries as I could carry, and then, remembering that there was an unused pair of hands some-where behind me, I bought some more, turned a corner and waited. I surprised him when he came round, and without asking I handed Rob the sack of squash and potatoes. He took it from me nervously.

'You will carry this for me, if you please, Rob,' I said.

'Oh, I couldn't, miss!' he said.

'You most certainly can,' I said, and walked off.

There was more to buy: flour and sugar and some other sundries for Mrs Dawes; flowers to brighten the drawing room and the downstairs; a game hen which John and I would have together the next evening. I returned to the confectioners and spared no expense on desserts. I purchased petits fours, and jam-filled fancies, and of course a good amount of the candied cherries. There were glazed apricots in the case, and I recalled that day when I had stood in that very spot, and heard Mr Rivers. 'The apricots are beautifully preserved,' he had said. Or at least he claimed to have said that, when I knew he had said something else. All of the dreadful business with him had yet to begin. I had not been on my guard, but I now knew the truth. The vile thing he had said that day came rushing back to me, and deep within me I understood that he had somehow been involved in Mr Luckhurst's death.

We went home, with Rob trailing behind me, and as I walked through the streets, I thought for the first time about Mr Rivers coursing those paths too. For when it all started, I had liked to think of Mr Rivers as I thought of John – as something that was mine, and mine in the house. But I had learned, to my great discredit, that Mr Rivers was not in my possession at all, but rather someone who belonged entirely to another world, making his way through it with his sinful routines, going from this alleyway to that passage, devising and effecting treachery. Where he went at night, where he walked, I hardly knew. But it was here, somewhere, in those dimly lit streets, past black-shadowed archways and evil-looking houses, and women with harsh voices who called out to him from their stoops. Yes, Mr Rivers, you've thought me a fool – a fool who could never envision you here, doing the deplorable kinds of things you do. You think that I do not see you – all of you – but I do. And the secrets you've kept, and the things you have done, all in the 'service' of protecting my family, you shall do no more, because you are not of this family. The truth is that you never could be.

At home, I set the groceries down beneath the portico, and waited for Rob to catch up with me.

'If he should see me, miss—' Rob began.

'And what if he does, Rob?' I said. 'It won't matter any more.'

And that was true, because in another day's time, Mr Rivers would have no say.

Rob set the sack he was carrying for me down on the porch. I opened one of my bags and pulled out two tartlets.

'Now you take these, sweet Rob, and you run around to the back gate. I shall be leaving no more today, so your work is done, and you can rest easy.'

The boy took the sweets from me and ran round the corner, and Susan opened the door for me and helped me inside.

'Miss!' she said. 'You disappeared before I could get myself together to accompany you.'

'It's all right,' I replied. 'You had much to do this morning, and there is much more that we still have to do.'

'Miss?' she questioned.

Susan – faithful Susan. The only one I could trust with the plan.

'We need to ready the upstairs,' I said.

'Where?' she asked.

'The third floor – the green room.'

'Master Tom's old room?'

'Precisely.'

Susan frowned.

'By the end of tomorrow,' I said, 'the room must be ready. The linens must be fresh. The coals must be burning. The curtains washed and re-hung. And some of these flowers to add some cheer.'

'But miss,' Susan protested, 'that room is so damp. And then the smell—'

I stopped her.

'And that is why we must take the greatest pains to freshen it. No one has slept in that room since poor Tom. It has suffered from such neglect all these years, and all of it my fault. I should have known better. But no matter. We can do it. And the room will be bright again.'

'But miss—' Susan continued.

'Please, Susan – just do as I say. You and I both will spend all of tomorrow reviving the room together, and when we are finished we shall prepare for the next vital undertaking.'

'And what's that, miss?'

'Moving my brother.'

The thing about the paper in Tom's room was that it was of a green that constantly changed – or at least it seemed to. In the bright sun of morning its blue pigments were more pronounced, and at times the resulting colour was a watery aquamarine; as the day progressed though, and the sun moved round the house, that lovely, spring-like hue deepened into something darker and more foreboding. On the surface, the pattern was not terribly elaborate, but if you looked closer, you could detect so many different shapes that made up the design. The pattern was not one of fruit or leaves or flowers exactly, but something that suggested all of those things at once. There was much to see in the paper if you spent enough time looking. And Tom had seen so much.

Susan was indeed right about the smell up there – something like a dead mouse but not quite as strong. The room was damp, on the north side of the house, with only the one window to brighten it. But the room, relative to the others, was also quite small, and the coal stove in there heated the space beautifully. And in the evening, when the fire was going, and the candles were lit, it was the cosiest room of all the rooms in our house.

The room was still every bit Tom's.

When I think back to how I took care of him during those years, I am angry. For if I had known then what I know now, things might have gone differently. My poor brother – how those phantoms came after him every night. How I was unwilling to see it. He gasped and he cried and I should have known. I looked into his eyes – they were telling me. His soft white skin, his forehead perspiring. His little voice calling me, breaking.

But I was a girl, and the message was unclear. And I could not understand what they were saying.

Those poor children.

The room was rarely used – always locked up – and so it was dusty and dank, with cobwebs in every corner. More than anything else it needed fresh air, and so I lifted the sash as high as I could, and let the cool air stream into the chamber. The day was not freezing when Susan and I were cleaning, and so the window could remain open and freshen everything as we worked. We scrubbed the floors, though we did not need to, and polished every groove of the trim around the mantel. We washed the curtains in the morning and had them hanging up again by midday. I made up the bed with crisp sheets and soft blankets. My little Tom had always looked so small in that wondrous bed.

By evening, the room was once again alive. The leaves in the paper once again growing.

'Tomorrow,' I whispered.

'Oh, miss . . .' Susan said.

And then she collapsed into me, and let out a soft sob. I held her, and a tear came into my eye too.

'Thank you, Susan,' I said. 'You've never failed me.'

'Oh, miss,' she repeated, 'not a day goes by . . .'

'I know,' I said. 'Me too.'

We held each other for some moments and then I released her, and we stood together in the centre of the room, our eyes wet, the walls dark and blurry. The room was now a different room in the fading December light. The last bits of sun struggled to survive in the approaching cold.

'Now tomorrow,' I said, 'just before dawn, you will do exactly as we have discussed.'

Susan nodded.

'You will take Mrs Dawes and my brother, and you will go. All will be well. Mr Ismay will have arranged everything.'

'I am so fearful of leaving you here, miss,' Susan protested. 'Leaving you alone with—'

'You have nothing to fear,' I said. 'You must trust in what I'm saying.'

Susan nodded, relented.

'This is the only way,' I said.

I squeezed Susan's hand – that strong, faithful hand – and dismissed her so that she could go downstairs to help Mrs Dawes prepare dinner. I remained there and listened. A soft wind was coming in, and brought with it a smattering of sounds from the city. A pair of footsteps on the pavement. The jingle of a horse's reins. A child's laugh. A distant whistle. A whole world encroaching in with the cold.

I walked over and slammed shut the window.

I was ready.

XXI

ALL WENT WELL the next morning, and by dawn I was alone in the house. Of course, my brother had protested against the idea of leaving, more, I think, because he did not want to leave me alone than because he was afraid to leave. But I had left him no choice: I had told him that he must go away – that he simply could not be there the next time that Mr Rivers arrived. My brother looked at me strangely – he knew, but did not know. I said nothing. John left with Susan, his nightmares chasing him as he went.

I watched the light swell from dark grey to bluish purple. Time passed, the morning grew, and the December sun streamed into the drawing room. The sky became bright, and while the night had been cold, the morning was, on that day, like a morning in May. I had remained at John's bedside for most of the night and had not slept. And so I was tired, even at that hour when I should have been most alert. But I was not worried, for I had the rest of the day to finish; Mr Rivers would not be coming until dinner.

What it was to linger in that house – my house, our house, father's house – on that last day is hard to describe, especially when the day was so lovely, and what was about to happen was so unspeakable. But strangely, that contrast was a perfect metaphor for everything that had ever happened to our family. All those beautiful days and months and years, surrounded by the luxuriousness of the company, while underneath a guileful sickness festered. They had been telling us all along – crying out and telling us – but no one, it seemed, wanted to hear it. And that was my fault, because I was the one person who could have heard.

That is, if I had chosen to listen.

I tidied the house for the rest of the afternoon, and surveyed all the rooms as one surveys troops in the battlefield. In the kitchen, Mrs Dawes had removed all of the perishable supplies from the cupboards. Some spices remained, and some parchment paper, and the large roll of trussing string, but other than those items and the melting ice in the ice-box, the downstairs was sufficiently empty. Upstairs, in the dining room, the table was not set for dinner, but rather polished brilliantly like a mirror, with mother's candelabra at the centre. By mid-afternoon, the weather had begun to turn, and a greyer light seeped in to coat the red fronds of that room's carnivorous paper. I continued through the ground floor and closed all of the panelled shutters, ensuring that every window was latched shut before I did so.

Upstairs there was mother's room, and my room, and John's room . . . the beds all made, the curtains and panels open, the items on every shelf and table and mantel all dusted and tidied. I walked through John's room, sat and thought, and went upstairs. Mother's room, with its birds and great pieces of furniture that never moved, still had the smell of mother's dressing gowns – a soft, powdery smell that lingered in the air even though her powder box hadn't been opened since she died. I went across the hall, and stepped into my room, and the starkness of my plain pink walls struck me as it never had before. So many years ago, mother had chosen that colour for me, had rid my room of the little flying creatures that gave me nightmares. And the colour had, over the years, somehow managed to follow me, and find its way into all sorts of things that brought me unexpected comfort: the blush of a doll's cheek, the icing on a petit four, the remains of strawberry juice mixed with cream, the pale blossom of a fresh camellia.

The hall was quiet, the clock ticked. I stood at the top of the stairs, looking down. I had spent so much of these recent years of my life going down those stairs, to John. I remembered the day we moved him into father's study, so that he could be closer to the ground floor, and thus would not have to travel as far to the dining room. I was sixteen. It was two years after Tom. And John had returned home from school, unable to finish the term. At first, we had thought something must have happened to him while he was away, but his weakness, even then, pointed to something that had always been there, always growing. Having lost Tom so recently, we naturally thought we'd lose John as well. We almost did. The doctors could not make head or tail of his condition. Mother was no help and cried into her handkerchief more than anything else. And I knew that if we lost John, we would likely lose her too.

But we didn't, and John moved into father's study, and while everything was not fine, it was acceptable. That staircase – I looked down upon it, upon the evenness of its treads, and the regularity of its angles. My feet had mastered it, going up and down at all hours, to John, and then back to sleep. It was true, as Susan was often known to have said, that if the builders had taken half as much care with back staircases as they did with front ones, there would have been many more like her still alive and walking amongst us.

I continued tidying for the rest of the day, until the sun started setting, and I went up – or maybe it was down – to John's room for one of the very last times. The bed was made with the beautiful counterpane that had been handed down from father's mother, and in the yellowing light, father's wallpaper was a swamp of things gnarled and twisted. John's room, as I have described, was the strange concoction of a bedroom and an office. And there, clean at last, and rid of all its papers, was father's desk, its smooth and green embossed leather surface darkening into a black pool in the dusk. I sat on John's bed for one final time, and breathed in, thinking how impossible it was that he was not in it. The window was locked. I scanned the walls and the ceiling. Henry's cage still stood in the corner, empty.

I rose, smoothed the counterpane, and returned to the ground floor. I wanted Mr Rivers to let himself in, so before the hour when he was to arrive, I left the front door ajar. A thin line of cold air breathed in through the crack. But the door was heavy, and the door stayed in place.

And then at last the time did come, and the whole plan called me up. And for a moment, perhaps the longest moment that ever held me, I saw the whole thing come crashing down upon me. Mr Rivers a giant. Mr Rivers triumphing after all – throwing me to the ground, calling me a fool, and taking everything that belonged to me, just as he had always intended. He had once told me that I had needed protection, and he was right. But what he did not know was that I could protect myself in ways that he never could have imagined.

He could not win.

I lit the lamps on the ground floor and ascended the stairs. I lit the hallway, then John's room, then my room, then mother's. The whole house was aglow as if in anticipation of a party. I wanted Mr Rivers to see everything.

At last I reached the third-floor hall and lit the small lamp there too. For the smaller rooms and Susan's room – these doors were open. But the door to Tom's room I closed and locked. I tied the key to a long ribbon, and hung the ribbon round my neck.

I lit a candle, and stood in the dark at the very end of the long hall. Ahead of me, in the centre, the main staircase, where, after tearing through the whole house, the beast would have no choice but to emerge. And to my side, the dark shaft of the intractable back staircase, no light upon it, going down, down, down. I stood and waited, and for once there was no one crying out, and the walls were as still as the darkness. I waited for minutes that passed by like hours, until at last I heard the closing and the click of the front door, down below.

If he knew, which was of course always a possibility and my greatest fear, he would dart straight up to the third floor, seize me, and all might be over. But if he were forced to creep through the house, room by room, little by little, observing with each step all the emptiness I had laid before him, his anger would mount, his fury would boil over, and by the time he reached me, he would be ready.

I listened.

There were steps down below – miles away. He saw the dining-room table with no plates or cutlery, no serving dishes on the sideboard, no smell from the kitchen. I had lit mother's candelabra before I had come up, and it was laughing – laughing at Mr Rivers with each flame.

'Miss Braithwhite?' I heard, again as if from the greatest distance.

Towards the back of the house, perhaps the morning room –

'Miss Braithwhite?'

Then footsteps, the staircase, the first-floor landing – John's bedroom.

And then, something between a gasp and a cry that was not human.

A race of footsteps up the next flight of stairs – to my room, and into mother's. And then the most horrible shattering of glass. He had taken up something – perhaps one of the lamps – and thrown it straight into the mirror.

The third flight of steps. There was almost nothing between us now. He knew I was up there – I had to be – and so he did not run. He collected himself, though it was clear he was not fine. In his wildest fancies he never imagined this could happen. I, Lucy Braithwhite, was taking everything he had ever wanted. Everything he thought he deserved.

His steps approached – like an animal's – inexplicably softer as they drew closer.

And then, of a sudden, he leapt from the staircase and into the hall, his face so hellish and so appalling that even the most delirious dream could never have conjured it. And yet, even in that, even in that *evil*, there was the strangest and most joyful glitter in his eyes. An incongruous joy that mixed with his malice to alter the aspect of his whole face.

His eyes bore down upon me. He could have been on me at once, but he waited.

'Where is he?' he said.

The vampire was hungry.

I held my candle, gave no reply. Mr Rivers glanced at Tom's door.

'Mr Braithwhite?' he called.

Then he ran to it, tried its knob, and finding that he could not open it, began pounding.

'Mr Braithwhite!' he called out again.

He turned to me, and gazed at what dangled below my bosom.

'You will give me that key or I will beat down this door.'

Try as he could, he could not hide his rage. The man was trembling, and had grown pallid.

'You're mad,' he said. 'Insane.'

His eyes were fire. He understood what I was doing, and he hated me.

Then he whispered something terrible under his breath, and his monstrous body made to move towards me. But before he could lunge, I slipped into the back stairwell and shot down, being careful to avoid the places that I knew would be his downfall. His rage and his confidence would condemn him to carelessness, and for once, even with everything so manifestly about him, Mr Rivers would not be able to see.

I reached the bottom landing and looked up, just as he was turning the corner into the stairwell. He gripped the door frame and took in the maddening sight of me. We studied each other – one predator eyeing its prey.

I am looking up at you again and I see you, Mr Rivers, about to leap down towards me in your passion and your rage. You've been hateful and you've been foolish. Yes, that has been your downfall. You've disrespected our family's house, and all those who've lived within it.

Then all at once he was heaving – galloping towards me like an animal. He was practically stumbling down, his face darkened with rage. He could not catch his breath. And then, suddenly – it happened. But what happened I could not exactly see. The walls breathed out and Mr Rivers fell – headlong – over himself and down the rest of the steps.

I moved back just far enough for him to miss my feet. I held my candle. The flame flickered. I looked up the tunnel towards the light.

His head had smashed hard against one of the walls as he tumbled. There was a mark there from the wound, nothing else.

And now the crumbled man was before me – a version of Mr Rivers that I never imagined I'd see. He lay there on the ground, lifeless as a discarded puppet. And one of his legs was resting at the most horrible, unnatural angle.

I waited. Nothing moved, and nothing came.

'Mr Rivers,' I said.

But the man did not stir.

I repeated the name again – the name that had meant so much.

His stillness and his silence filled me with apprehension and disbelief. In my mind, he rose up, shook off his pain, and strangled me. Resolute as I had become, there was still something in me that refused to believe that anything could defeat him. And yet, here he was, a mere pile of broken bones, his legs bent, his head bloody, even the skin of his hands torn.

'Mr Rivers.'

I did not want to leave him, and yet what I needed to do next I could not do alone. And so, having no choice, I did leave Mr Rivers, and ran to the window at the other side of the hall. The dark had almost set in, and the street lamps had been lit, and in the fading twilight I could discern Rob's shadow down below.

I opened the window and called his name, but the boy only crouched closer to the back gate when he heard me.

'Rob!' I called again.

Still nothing.

Then, finally, upon the third call, the boy moved out into the open. He looked up towards the window, his face indistinguishable in the dark, and I shouted for him to go around to the front door and come inside. But he shook his head, afraid as ever, and worried his hands as he shifted.

'Rob,' I called firmly. 'You must do as I say at once. I will not ask you again.'

The boy stood still.

'At once,' I repeated, and closed the window.

I rushed back down the hallway and turned into the back stairwell. And there Mr Rivers was standing, his head bloodied, his eyes aflame! The man reached out to grab me, but I violently jumped back, only in doing so I stumbled and fell to the floor. My head hit the ground just shy of the iron doorstop. I was stunned, a slight pain already beginning to throb. I shook my head, rolled to my side, and was moving to pick myself up again when Mr Rivers pounced upon me and pinned me to the ground.

His face was the face of a demon. His eyes were fire – pure hatred, evil. I struggled, but the hands were already about my neck, closing harder and harder upon me. He was choking out my breath – I would not win this battle. I grabbed his wrists, pried his hands. But the demon was too strong.

His grip tightened as I thrashed beneath him, and I gasped and choked for air. The blood from the wound on the side of his head trickled down and spattered around my eyes.

The air was going out of me and I could not fight him for long. My fading vision saw one thing: the eyes of hatred. I had never seen such hatred, such determination, such abhorrence in another pair of human eyes before. The harm those eyes alone could do – so fierce in their rage and their power.

My life was gone. The monster was killing me. The monster was killing what it hated.

I thought of John. I thought of Tom. I thought of the hills and the house in Devon. I would not survive to see it again – to see any of them again. My plan had failed. John and Susan would perhaps be safe for a short while; that is, until Mr Rivers found them. They would never have time to suspect that he would be coming for them, and then Mr Rivers would do what he had destined himself to do. He would come in and take everything that he felt belonged to him. He would possess everything forever. I would not be there to protect them.

The light was going out for me. I had gambled and I had failed. I could not blame anyone for my foolishness and my failure. I was the only one to blame – for everything. My last resort was to surrender. I began to loosen my grip, to resist my impulse to thrash. The hands tightened ever harder, and I could no longer breathe. I saw John, I saw Tom. Their faces lined with tears. I saw all of them – calling me, reaching for me.

And then, a blow – a horrible sound. The grip loosened, and the full weight of the man was suddenly off me.

I gasped, still choking, and tried to regain my breath. And there was Rob, standing with the iron doorstop in his hand.

I panted. Rob was still. After a few moments I sat up. I reached out my hand and he came over to me. I held his hand. It was soft and warm.

Next to us, on the ground, Mr Rivers lay unconscious, a small pool of blood beneath the deep wound on the side of his head.

Rob was trembling.

'Rob,' I said, lifting myself up and standing next to him.

Rob dropped the doorstop.

'Oh . . .' he whispered.

I pulled him close to me and I kissed him. I gripped his hand.

'Rob,' I said, 'sweet Rob. The time has come.'

'Oh, miss!' he exclaimed, 'I must go and fetch one of the doctors!'

He wrenched his hand away and made to leave, but I grabbed him, and pulled him close to me again.

'No, Rob,' I said. 'The time has come, and you must listen. You must help me take your master up these stairs.'

'But miss . . .' Rob protested. 'I'm sorry!'

'Do not be sorry,' I said. 'We must get him into bed. You must listen to me, Rob. This is the only way.'

I went over to the body and made to lift the legs myself, and when I looked up at Rob, he was staring.

'Rob!' I commanded.

And with that he reawakened, and obeyed, and rushed over to help me. He put his own arms under the arms of his master, and tugged up the first step, and so the body followed his path. In front of him, I lifted the legs and guided the body. Rob was strong, but so was I, and step by step we drew him up.

'Take care, Rob,' I advised. 'The steps are uneven.'

We reached the top, and dragged Mr Rivers all the way down the hall to the door of Tom's room. I took the key from my neck and undid the lock. The room was warm and comfortable from the coals.

We pulled Mr Rivers across the carpet and lifted him into the bed. Mr Rivers moaned as we shifted him. Rob did what he did without thinking, but there was more working upon the poor boy than he ever could have realised. He helped me as one who can do nothing else but help, though his anxiousness remained with him until the end.

At last, when I had Mr Rivers fully tucked into the bed, the sheets tight about him, the pillow now stained with blood, I sat Rob in one of the chairs by the window and kneeled before him.

'A doctor, miss—' Rob began.

But I stopped him.

'Now, Rob,' I said. 'This is the best place for your master at this moment. I want you to look at me, Rob. This is the best place for him, do you hear?'

I raised his chin with my finger. The boy looked over at Mr Rivers, then at me, and nodded.

'This is the best place for him,' I repeated, 'and this is where he must stay. You know what house this is – isn't that right, Rob?'

'Yes, miss.'

'And you know who I am, yes?'

'Yes.'

'And you know, Rob, that I know what is best – even for you.'

Rob looked down.

'I'm sorry, miss.'

I pulled from my skirt the money and the note I had prepared for him.

'I want you to take this,' I said, pressing the money into
his hand. 'Use it for cabs if you need it to get where you
are going. Or use it to buy yourself food tonight, or in the
morning. It is yours, Rob. And this paper – are you able to
read what is upon it?'

I handed Rob the paper with the place and the schedule.
He looked at it.

'A little, miss,' he said. 'Not everything.'

'But do you see where I need you to go?'

'Yes.'

'Very well then, Rob. You will meet me at the station first
thing in the morning, and you will be ready. The train leaves
at dawn. You will be with me now. Do you understand?'

'But—'

I seized both of his hands – his handsome, innocent
hands.

'Your master shall remain here and we shall both be far
away from him.'

'But where, miss?' he said.

'Very far away.'

Rob looked over at the window – the closed window that
kept out the air.

'Miss,' he said, his face softening, his hands holding onto
mine.

'You know who I am, Rob, and you know that I shall take
care of you – always. And as long as you are with me, no
one will ever be able to hurt you again.'

XXII

AND NOW I must bring an end to these difficult pages, for I have put down the whole matter as it needed to be told. We are here, I believe, as the result of certain inevitabilities that drive us, but also as the result of what we choose to see, and what we do not.

The house in Devon has very little paper. It is a country house with lime-washed walls that are chalky and devoid of all colour. There are almost no patterns, but the patterns that do emerge are lovely – soft shadows of white and off-white and grey that blend to form the ghostliest of landscapes. Later, after we had all been settled for some months, old Mrs Dawes, in her final hours, looked for something in those walls. She was searching, it seemed, for something from the London house – something that was still there for her, even though it was not there. Not that Mrs Dawes had ever spent much time upstairs, of course. But the other house had been part of her, and she a part of it, and in the end perhaps there was no escaping what she had once seen there.

The house in Devon does not receive visitors – except for Mr Ismay, who might come once or twice a year. He has been such a help to me and my brother, and without him I don't know how we'd manage. He is a good man and an honest man, but he is not a brilliant man, and so under him and a few of the others, the company has already changed. The company will survive, because the company cannot but survive. There is a vision of it that the world could never do without. But it is different somehow – lesser. There are those who are not there, and those who remain, who walk the stairwells and the aisles, and leave their subtle mark. John's mark is one of those marks, for in the end his papers were all corrected and in order. But he is much changed, my brother, and his mind needs rest. We've decided that it would be best for him to no longer be involved.

The house in Devon is a very simple house, and life is simpler for us here. It is our family's house – familiar – with memories all around. I care for John, for that is my greatest wish, and we have only Susan and Rob for our company. My brother, not quite weak but not strong, accompanies me to those places where we roamed long ago – over the hills and around the boulders and through the heather that coloured our youth. For they are the same fields – they are always the same – as are the bogs and the kestrels and the butterflies and the linnets. There is a hill that I see there, and the grass along its ridge forms a pattern – the pattern of a thousand teeth, the bottom jaw of a ferocious mouth. And above that line, somewhere in the blue through which the crows might fly, or the grey, or the white, or whichever colour the sky decides to pronounce, there is nothing but air – that clean and crisp air – that wants nothing, that hides nothing, that has nothing.

For so long I wanted to see them again. I envisioned them walking in an uneven line along the ridge – the children I could never quite recognise. They could have been any children from the story I have lived, poor or rich, short or tall, full or hungry, clean or dirty. They could have been Tom. They could have been John. They could have been a hundred other children I never knew. We could have been any of them, because we were all one, and without one another there would have been no hope for any of us. The mists come in and blur the hills and the sky, and the night air grows heavy with the smell of damp and decay. And though, through the mist, all around seems vast and barren, there is never a time when shifts and changes are not coming. The owls screech, the bitterns boom. In the morning, the air clears, and I see them.

The memory of the other house is no longer with me – or at least I try not to let it be. It is not a memory that I want for myself or any of us, and there is nothing there that I want to dream of. For yes, it is still there, stubbornly standing on our street, locked up, the sun coming in on both sides of the great drawing room. I retain the only key, and it is here with me in Devon, asleep in the top drawer of the linen press, alongside the billhook that mother once mentioned.

What I see there, though, if I do chance to dream of the London house . . . what I hear there is silence, as evening darkens the rooms. Only the shadows creep into the rooms from the outside, and as night arrives and the fires burn hotter, the colours fade wearily out of things.

A cold rain starts. The whole house burns with warmth. I am sitting there watching him breathe.

He stirs.

The eyes open, just barely. The candle is lit, and he sees me. He looks small in the bed. The slightest movement, a struggle.

The coals glow, and I imagine them fading into black. The cold and the damp settling back in.

He breathes. The eyes widen. His eyes fix on the wall.

'Please . . .' he whispers.

But the word is rough, the throat dry. I pour some water for him from the pitcher, and hold the glass to his lips. He sips. His lips make a pathetic, desperate sound. I let him take the water. Then I put the glass down.

'There is enough here for you for some days,' I say. 'And I have dosed it sufficiently for your pain.'

His head moves, but he is too weak to let out a moan. He looks at me, and to my wonder, the eyes have lost their sparkle. He knows what I am about to do, and in his eyes there is not fear. Instead there is something subtler there, like sorrow – or resignation.

And what is he trying to say to me with those eyes? Those eyes that always said so much? Something, perhaps, that is unexpectedly full of understanding – or even kindness?

It did not need to happen, the eyes seem to be saying. *None of it needed to happen.*

And yet, all of it did.

He moves his mouth, tries to say my name. I touch his lips. I do not let him. It is much too late for regret, apologies.

'Please don't—' I say.

Please don't tell me you would have made them better.

He looks at me again, and the face that once captivated me is now distorted. It is filthy. He is still, and as we gaze at each other, the eyes grow deep, and familiar. They are the eyes of a child I once saw on the moors. Or at least I think they are, if such a child there ever were, for they are now full of the same fear and desperation. The eyes of a child lost, and forgotten.

I offer more water, but the lips do not take it. The eyes are staring – staring at the paper.

I rise, smooth my skirt, and move towards the fire. The green walls are black in these last hours before dawn. The rain is coming – the damp, the winter. I approach the mantel and poke at the coals.

Some faint sound blows, and I hear it.

'The window is quite loose and can be an annoyance in the wind,' I say.

Perhaps he is hearing me. Perhaps not.

'I've nailed it shut.'

And now, not looking at me, but still gazing into the paper, a sigh escapes him – a sigh that tells me that he knows. For that had always been the most remarkable thing about him. He knew. It had been impossible for him not to know.

He closes his eyes – sleeps quietly in the bed.

'I'm sorry,' I say.

And the glow from the fire shows me.

I look around at the walls and the shadows one last time. Tom's walls – the walls of our family.

I hear his shortened breaths, and I move out of the room.

I close the door. I turn the key.

I lock the door.

Acknowledgements

For help with the development of this novel at its various stages, the author would like to thank: John Bowen, Manoah Bowman, Nick de Somogyi, Jacques de Spoelberch, JoAnna Giltner, Jim Porteous, Richard Porteous, Jason Rudy, Jeremiah Rusconi, and Charlotte Seymour. Special thanks to Hollis Seamon, from beginning to end; to Jade Chandler, for transformation; and to Joseph Geller – for everything.